THE
SECRET
LIBRARY

A NEW KEEPER

J. C. GILBERT

Books by J. C. Gilbert

The Secret Library

Book One: A New Keeper
Book Two: Call of Kuyr
Book Three: The Spaces Between
Book Four: The Last Garden
Book Five: Seas of Baast
Book Six: Ash (Coming soon in 2020)

Secret Library Short Reads (Read between A New Keeper and Call of Kuyr)

Book Zero: Grimm Tidings
Book One: Journey to the Christmas Lands
Book Two: The Paper Witch (Coming soon in 2020)

The Cowboy Karen

Book One: Asteroid Jazz
Book Two: Tomato, Tomato
Book Three: Silvery Moon

Bounty Hunter Academy

Book One: Witchcraft and Weaponry (Coming soon in 2020)

THE SECRET LIBRARY: A NEW KEEPER

Copyright © 2020 Jonathan Gilbert

All rights reserved.

Published by Tardigrade House 2019

Auckland, New Zealand

This is a work of fiction. Any similarity between the characters and situations within its pages and places or persons, living or dead, is unintentional and co-incidental.

Cover Design by saraoliverdesign.com

For Sara

OK, I can do this. I just needed to distract myself, so I
searched my brain for something unrelated to ... and ...
... IV

CHAPTER 1

A hedgehog lives in my heart. Like, an actual live hedgehog.

We are not friends.

His hobbies include burrowing into my stomach, clawing at my arteries, thumping on my blood pump, and turning off my lungs.

His name is Hank. I started calling him that after watching a video about giving your anxiety a name.

Right now, I needed Hank to leave. I was the first student to arrive at Mrs. Taylor's class. I knew that if I came any later, then I simply wouldn't be able to make it to my desk.

The room was stale with the smell of old stationary and baked dust. My chair screeched as I pulled it out. I sat down and tried to breathe. The classroom slowly filled with students. Now that I was seated, I wished that I stayed home.

Hank tore out my lower intestine.

OK, I can do this. I just needed to think of something else. I searched my brain for something unrelated to school. I tried to remember the last thing I saw on TV.

The face of Benedict Cumberbatch came to mind. Sherlock Holmes wouldn't be feeling this way. He would be able to rationalize his emotions as just the chemical signals from an outdated warning system.

He probably would have deleted Hank. Or trained him to run errands.

Lucky Sherlock.

I shuffled in my chair. So maybe I didn't have to do this? There was still time to leave. Leaving would feel wonderful.

But what if I ran into Mrs. Taylor in the hall? She would want to know where I was going, especially as class was due to start.

Hank headbutted something soft and full of nerve endings.

I liked Mrs. Taylor, I really did. She was kind and read a lot. She told us all on the first day of class that she was a Hufflepuff. We were on the same wavelength, and that was pretty cool.

But once a year, she transformed from my kind and geeky English teacher to a torturer. She became this ruthless and cunning puppet master, and I her unwilling puppet.

On cue, she walked in and smiled as if nothing were the matter, as if this were just another day.

OK, so I couldn't outright leave. But maybe I could leave once class started? People go to the bathroom all the time, don't they? I could go to the bathroom. That would be a totally reasonable and appropriate thing to do.

And then I could just not come back.

Hank liked this idea too. Good.

Of course, then people might wonder why I was in the

bathroom for so long. What if Mrs. Taylor sent someone after me? Definitely not good.

I pictured Amy and Claire, the two 'popular' kids knocking on the door of the cubical. 'What *are* you doing in there, Alex?'

I flinched as Hank bit my optic nerve, and the image was forced from my mind.

No. I worked too hard for this. I had to stay. I had to see this through. I only needed to get rid of my little problem, and then everything would be fine.

"Alright, class," said Mrs. Taylor, voice raised. She stood at her post in front of the white-board. She had written three names there: Finn, Jessica, and Alexandria.

My heart skipped a beat.

That's me, by the way. I am Alexandria when written down and Alex when spoken aloud. I have difficulty saying my own name sometimes. It's kind of embarrassing, tbh.

"So today we will be continuing on with oral presentations. Now I want you all to show today's speakers the same consideration that they have shown you over the last week. Finn? You wanna come on up?"

Finn, a lanky boy with light hair, tumbled to the front of the class.

So I was going to be last. That wasn't so bad. I'll just have to sit here. Waiting. Me and Hank. This is fine.

I felt dizzy.

Leaning forward, I dug my elbows into my desk and pressed my palms into my skull.

Concentrate. I needed to concentrate. Then an idea struck me. I would sketch while the other two were speaking. People might think it was rude, but sometimes anxiety makes you rude. It was better to appear a little rude than be forced to hang out with my rodent problem through the whole class. It was for the best.

Finn started talking, but he might as well have been speaking in Simlish for all I understood.

I forced my pen to paper and started drawing. I drew what I pretty much always drew. I liked to start with the eyes, making them fierce, capturing that cold and ancient intelligence. I then used that start to guide the position of its jaw and the shape of its head. Its torso and its legs started to emerge, now a tail. It was the final touch that always gave me the biggest thrill: its wings, unfurled and unafraid.

I locked eyes with the dragon for a moment.

"Thank you, Finn. That was very insightful."

Hank grabbed my heart with two tiny hands and buried his face into it, screaming.

What was I going to do? I couldn't go up like this!

I pulled out my cue cards and tried to read over them one more time. The words which I had crafted with care over many nights of work didn't appear to make any sense.

Maybe I don't speak English? Would Mrs. Taylor buy that?

Probably not.

Sweat from my palms dampened the edge of my cue cards, making them fold in my hands. I tried to flick through them, but they stuck together.

Breathe, just breathe.

Jessica looked confident. I had no idea what she was saying, but she seemed fine. I wouldn't be fine. I would freeze, and then everyone would give me that 'trying to be encouraging, but really I have no idea why you are failing so bad' look.

I hated that look.

I glanced back down at my dragon. I pictured him chasing Hank away. Not burning him to a crisp or anything. That would be murder. I only wanted to scare him a little.

I could do this. It was only one tiny speech. I would go up there and make it happen. I am a human being with the capabilities of most other human beings.

At least the capabilities of Jessica.

Jessica smiled as the class clapped. She looked relieved as she took her seat.

Only one tiny speech.

"Alexandria, you're up."

CHAPTER 2

I didn't move. I sat there, staring at my sketch, vaguely curious about how time felt when it was on the end of a pin.

"Alex, it's your turn now," said Mrs. Taylor.

"I can't," I said. My voice wavered.

"Yes, you can. Come on up," she said. She was trying to be encouraging.

My eyes met hers. I saw that fading light, that shift from where people think you are just like everyone else to where they discover that you aren't. You are different.

"I forgot," I squeaked.

All eyes were on me now. Too silent.

"You forgot your cue cards?" Mrs. Taylor frowned, clearly confused.

"I don't have any. I forgot about it."

Hank was holding his breath. There was no random giggling here today. I had the stage, and I was here to make a fool of myself.

"Everyone has to do a presentation, Alex."

I shrugged. I felt like I was five years old. I had no excuse. I wanted to tell Mrs. Taylor that I hadn't done it because it's just who I am. I just let people down. Her compassion made it worse.

"OK, well then. I'll have a talk with you after class. Who is next on the list - Jake? I don't suppose you are ready to do yours today?"

"Screw that," said Jake. The class erupted with laughter. Hank let out a sigh of relief, curled up, and went to sleep. It was over, and I had escaped.

I had escaped, but Hank had won.

***

When the bell rang for lunch, I scrambled out the door as fast as I could. There was no way I wanted to talk to Mrs. Taylor about my speech.

I felt that familiar mix of calm and shame. I just wanted to forget about the whole thing. Eventually, Mrs. Taylor would forget about it too, right?

I walked down the hall and outside, squinting as my eyes adjusted to the midday sun. It was early spring, and the sun was slowly breathing life back into the world.

I sat down at the octagonal bench where I always sat and pulled out a copy of Harry Potter and the Half-Blood Prince. Like most human beings, I had already read the series many times, but it was always worth a re-read.

This copy belonged to my mom. Our tastes were rarely the same, but we agreed when it came to important matters.

When I read, I can escape from all the thoughts and feelings associated with being a totally awkward human being. I can be an entirely different person, if only for a short time. Today I needed this as much as ever.

"How did your speech go?" asked Lilly, sitting down.

I breathed in and closed the book, keeping my place with a finger. Lilly was my best, and only, friend. She was bright-eyed, a tall girl with dark blond hair and enough enthusiasm to power a small nation.

"I don't want to talk about it," I said.

"Hank?"

"Yeah."

We had been friends for long enough for Lilly to have a pretty intimate understanding of Hank and his ways. She was probably the only person in the world who understood me and my quirks.

The school was alive with the vague and sometimes disturbing sounds of a few hundred kids pretending they were someplace else.

I focused on my book.

After about a page and a half, Lilly interrupted again. "Did you see my Insta?"

"Which one?"

"The one from today."

"I mean which account?"

Lilly had many.

"Oh, the coolasacantaloupe account. It's the one where I pair quotations from the transcendental poets with pictures of cantaloupe. Did I tell you about it? I started it on Sunday. Running out of free stock images of cantaloupe, though. I wanted to do cucumbers, but the handle was already taken."

"I'll have to check it out."

"What's that?" Lilly asked, pointing to my bag. I followed her gaze to my notebook, where a vicious looking dragon was poking his nose out.

"Nothing," I said. I moved to push the drawing back inside, out of sight.

I was too slow. Lilly seized the notebook and pulled it out of my reach. "Did you draw this?" she asked. She was staring at the paper.

"Yeah," I said. I could feel my cheeks growing warm.

"Don't look so serious! I like it. Can I have it?"

"What? No. Wait, you like it?"

"Yeah. I'm legitimately jealous of your talent, young lady."

"Thanks, I guess."

Lilly put the notebook down and spun around, her attention caught by something. She was like a squirrel. "Did you see that?" she asked.

"See what?"

"I could have sworn I saw a sword in that guy's bag."

"Like an actual hacky stabby kind of sword?" I stretched my neck to see where she was looking.

"Yes, a Viggo Mortensen' you have my sword' kind of sword."

"I don't see," I said, "he is walking away now."

"Should I ask him about it?"

"Ah-"

Lilly jumped up. "Hey, what's with the weapon?" she called.

His name was Darcy, a lanky boy with scruffy black hair and a face as serious as a pavement. I knew him, kinda. He lived on my street, and we always went to the same schools. He looked our way, eyes wide.

Hank woke up and stretched. I pulled the notebook towards me and closed it.

Lilly gestured for him to come over. He shuffled toward us.

"Hey," he said.

"Pretty casual for an armed man," said Lilly.

Darcy's gaze darted over his shoulder. "Could you keep it down? Please don't say anything about it." His expression was earnest.

"Gnorts, dude. I want to know where you got it 'cos I want one, that's all," said Lilly. Gnorts was Lilly's latest thing. She often experimented with new words and didn't much care that no one else knew what she meant by them.

"I made it," said Darcy.

"No, you didn't. No one makes swords."

"Look, I gotta go."

"You aren't going to go on some school rampage, are you?"

"Lilly!" I hissed. This conversation was stressing me out.

"Don't mind my friend," said Lilly, "she finds no joy in anything but reading."

I cringed.

"Then we should let her get back to her book," said Darcy.

"You shouldn't encourage her," said Lilly, "or we will never hear from her again."

"OK. Bye," said Darcy, retreating into the wilderness

of students.

"Ciao," said Lilly.

When Darcy was out of earshot, Lilly leaned in close. "Did you get that?" she asked in a conspiratorial whisper.

"Get what?"

"Sword-boy. He is totally into you, Alex."

"But he hardly even looked at me."

"Pointedly, one might say."

"So?"

"So people never ignore people without a good reason. Congratulations, Alex."

I gave Lilly a 'the world doesn't work the way you think it works' look.

She shook her head and smiled. "Come to mine after school? We still have one more season of Game of Thrones to re-watch."

"Sure," I said, mentally saying goodbye to another few hours of reading.

***

Watching TV with Lilly usually meant scrolling on social media while the show played. Lilly had a rumpus room all to herself. An eclectic array of movie posters and posters from bands which Lilly intended to 'get into' lined the walls.

The credits were opening on our third episode when I happened to glance at the time. It was five minutes to six.

"Shoot," I said. Mom always set dinner at six, and she usually got mad when I was late.

"What is it?"

"I gotta go."

"Wait, I wanna show you something." Lilly held up her phone, trying, and not succeeding, to keep it steady.

"I'm late."

"Just look!"

I took her phone. It was a picture of a man with a moth's head. He was getting distracted by a passing lamp while his girlfriend looked at him, offended by his wandering moth gaze.

I smiled. "Great, now I really have to go."

"Wait, wait, one more."

"No, I gotta go." My phone buzzed.

You coming home?

Mom phrased the text as a question but wielded it as a threat.

"This is important," she read aloud from her phone, "would you rather fight one horse-sized duck or a hundred duck-sized horses?"

"Sorry, what?"

"It's for research."

"Why am I fighting them?"

"Science."

"The horses sound pretty cute, so I guess I'll have to go with fighting a hundred duck-sized horses."

At that moment, Lilly's mom walked by, gave us a puzzled look, and then kept on walking.

"Let me get this straight, Alex Reed. You have chosen to fight one hundred duck-sized horses because they are cute? That's fudging sadistic," said Lilly, except she didn't say fudging.

"That's me, I guess."

"I fudging knew it."

"Now I have to go," I grabbed my bag and darted toward the door.

"See ya," called Lilly.

The evening was setting in around me as I fast-walked through the suburbs of Torbay. Yellow lit windows started to blink on in the shadowy houses. The skies were threatening rain, and I had not thought to bring a jacket with me. A single pioneer drop fell on the concrete in front of me. I looked about for somewhere to take cover.

Another drop fell, and then another.

Up ahead, there was a bus shelter. I hurried forward as the rain started to fall hard. My phone buzzed.

It looks like it is going to rain.

Thanks, Mom.

I made it to the shelter just as it really started to pour. The sound of the rain hitting the tin roof of the bus shelter was soothing. I would have appreciated it more if it weren't for the cold and the anticipation of coming home to a shirty mother.

Across from me, there was a row of shops. It was a collection of dry cleaners, stationers, and the like.

I knew this area very well. Having only one friend and a fondness for walking meant I came by here every other day. But today, something was out of place.

Through the failing light and the heavy rain, I could see a shop that I had not seen before. Between the post office and the grocers, there was a new shop. I could just make out the sign as *Fis Second Hand Books*.

A bookshop? But there was no bookshop in Torbay. I knew that. I was the book girl, and there were no bookshops in Torbay. Someone would have told me. It didn't look at all like a new shop either. It looked tatty, like something established in the '80s.

But this darn rain!

I resolved to check the store out as soon as it eased off. I was already late, but some things were worth investigating.

"This weather!" said a voice. I turned to see an elderly woman shuffling out of the rain. She slowly walked over and sat down beside me.

"Yeah," I said.

"Good walking weather, my husband would have said. He always liked spring."

The rain subsided a little and then came back stronger.

"Not too hot, not too cold," she continued.

"Hmm," I said. I wasn't trying to be rude, I just possess zero social skills.

I wanted to go now but didn't quite know how to disengage. It was an old lady trap.

"Can't walk in the summer because you get too uncomfortable."

I smiled and nodded.

"Can't walk in the winter because you will freeze. And these showers never last long, do they dear?"

"It's clearing up," I said.

"And here is my bus. Always the way."

"Oh, is it?" I asked.

Cringe.

"Thank you for listening to me natter on," she said.

I glanced up and saw a bus rounding the corner. It pulled up at the stop, and the old lady edged her way to the door.

"Bye," I said. I knew bye. Bye was easy.

I got up from my seat and waited for the bus to drive on. Its engine growled as it heaved away from the sidewalk.

But when it was gone, I saw something which made my heart skip a beat. I cast my gaze over the buildings before me and shook my head in disbelief.

The bookshop had vanished.

CHAPTER 3

I hurried across the road and walked right up to where I had seen the bookshop, between the post office and the grocery store. It was nowhere to be seen. The two stores shared a wall.

There was simply no room for a bookshop.

My mind spun, trying to account for this strangeness. I had seen the bookshop there. If I could trust my eyes, then I had seen it there.

I grew afraid.

It was dark now, and the street lamps had all switched on. I was about to start for home when I noticed something on the pavement. It was a business card, white, clean, and new. I bent down to pick it up.

Fis Second Hand Books. Opening Hours: Spring Showers and Summer Snow Storms.

It looked like some sort of joke. I turned it over. On the other side, there was an intricate black and white pattern made up of Labrador heads in silhouette. They formed a series of spirals.

I stuffed it into a pocket and began walking home. Once I was over the road, I took one look back, and then hurried on.

I got home just in time for dinner. My mom, dad, and little brother Jonny were all sitting around the dining table. I joined them and opened Harry Potter to where I had left off, clinging to the familiar.

"Really, Alex?" asked Mom.

The book was open in my left hand as I maneuvered a fork full of food toward my mouth with my right hand.

"What?" I mumbled.

"The book, Alex. Can't we just have family time without the book for once."

"I don't trust him," said Dad, watching the TV news from the dinner table.

"Who?" I asked.

"That Adams guy. I mean, look at him," said Dad, gesturing to the television. He connected with that particular piece of technology in a way that no one else I knew could.

"Really?" asked Mom, "is that how we are judging people now?"

"Look at him. He looks like he sells used cars or something. I feel like he is trying to sell me a car right now."

"Now that you mention it," said Mom, leaning into the madness.

"He has loads of overseas money, too, if you know what I mean."

I felt the tension of the room began to rise.

Aquaman gets to breathe underwater and command fish. Harry Potter gets to cast spells. Deadpool gets to break the fourth wall. My superpower was to sense the tension in the room. I shrank within myself.

"OK, let's just finish the conversation here, shall we?

I'm trying to eat," said Mom.

"I don't want to sound racist or anything-"

"Shppit."

"-but-"

"Can you just turn it off?"

"Can't do that, dear, sports next."

Realizing that family time was being revealed for the sham that it was, I slowly opened my book to where I was up to.

Mom shot me a look.

"I give up," she said and pulled out her mobile. "You OK, Jonny?" she asked my little brother. He was nine, but he was a young nine if you know what I mean.

"Yup," he said.

"You looked like you were off with the fairies."

Jonny always looked like he was off with the fairies. He looked at Mom with his eyes so wide that they were almost creepy. "Are fairies really real, Mom?"

I couldn't help but smile. Jonny was unique, that's for sure. He had this ability to erect a barrier between him and the rest of the world, shielding himself from anything which might mess with his balance. I think I used to have that, but somehow I lost it.

"Remember when we found the fairy circles in the forest?" asked Mom.

"I didn't see any fairies," said Jonny seriously.

"That's because they were hiding from Dad," I said.

"You beauty!" yelled Dad at some kind of sports.

"Can we go look for them tomorrow?" Jonny asked.

"Tomorrow is Tuesday, you will have to be at school

tomorrow."

"Oh," said Jonny. His face dropped.

"If the weather is fine, we can go on Saturday," said Mom. She looked at me, and I nodded. The fairy forest was awesome.

"Really?" asked Jonny, his eyes widening. He looked at me and then back to Mom, grinning. Jonny ate the rest of the meal humming along to himself. He ate his peas one at a time. Sometimes he took one up and split it in two, examining the inside before putting both halves in his mouth.

Yeah, he was a weird one, alright.

After dinner, I helped Mom with the washing up. I usually don't, but I kinda felt bad for family time or whatever. I liked helping Mom, but I didn't understand why we couldn't just use the dishwasher. Sure it didn't make things absolutely clean, but it got them close enough.

"Have you visited Grandma recently?" she asked.

I picked up another dish, wiped away the bubbles, and put it on the shelf with its friends. "I will soon." It really bothered me when Mom reminded me to do things like that. It's like she didn't think I was capable of thinking for myself or caring for people. I loved Grandma and loved visiting her. I just wished that, for once, I didn't have to feel guilty when I saw her.

"I was talking to your uncle," she said in that casual way, which people only use when their casualness is premeditated.

"Which one?" I asked.

"My brother, Jack."

Here we go. "Ah yip," I said, regretting that I didn't take

Harry Potter and hide upstairs.

"Well, I was talking to him, and he might have a summer job available, that is, if you need the money?"

That, of course, was mom-speak for you better start learning to get this money stuff soon, 'cos I ain't gonna pay for things forever.

"What kind of job?" I asked, hesitating.

"Data entry, I think. You will have to talk to him about it."

"So not working with other actual humans?"

"No, just you and the computer."

"That sounds pretty amazing," I said, deadpan.

"You are a worry," said Mom, "just give him a call and see if he has anything."

"I thought you said there was a job."

"You will have to call and see."

It was a beautifully choreographed awkwardness trap.

Thanks, Mom.

I could feel the anxiety build in my stomach as I tried to imagine calling up Uncle Jack. I mean, what is even the script here? Like, did he have a job for me or not? I guess it kind of made sense that Mom had first checked that there was a position, but was I supposed to pretend I didn't know that?

I didn't say anything more to Mom about it. In my over-analyzing thought storm, I completely forgot to tell her about the bookshop.

I'm not great with the whole 'other people' thing. I find it hard enough managing my own mental processes without taking other people into account.

Data entry over the summer would have been a godsend, which is a shame because there was no way I was going to be able to call my uncle.

I read for the rest of the night, trying to forget the day, forget the bookshop, and forget the data entry job. Once the lights were out, and I was tucked up in bed, my mind whirred along of its own accord. Was there a bookshop or wasn't there? Was I just going mad?

The strange business card sat on my bedside table, existing stubbornly.

CHAPTER 4

Lilly was used to me disappearing at lunchtime. She was one of those people who kind of knew everyone, so she never had to sit by herself. I needed alone time. The school, in general, was a sea of sound and awkward situations just waiting to be stumbled over.

I retreated into the school library. I didn't read there in general because there was a lot of distraction.

You would think that a library would be quiet, but this place was pseudo-quiet. The whispering was every so often broken with a 'sorry miss,' a moment of silence, and then more whispers.

I tried to get there early so that I could sit at the most secluded table. This meant that I wouldn't be eating until later.

I sat down at my favorite seat, pulled out my book, and began to read. I hadn't been reading long when a casual glance upwards led to eye contact with a person across the room from me. It was Darcy.

Hank kicked my left lung.

I wasn't sure if he had been there when I sat down or if he had sat across from me deliberately. I hoped that it wasn't deliberate because that was super creepy. I smiled at him weakly and tried to get back into my book.

I shifted in my seat.

Knowing he was there was distracting. I considered moving seats. What if he thought I was avoiding him? Or worse, what if he moved too?

I had to leave the library.

I put my book back in my shoulder bag and walked toward the exit, trying to look as casual as possible. I smiled at Darcy as I passed, but he wasn't looking.

Super awkward.

There was only one place that properly met my requirements for solitude. Over the sports field out the back of the school, up a small bank, there was a collection of trees. It was technically out of bounds, but it had served me well as an escape in the past.

I called it the sanctuary.

There was only one problem. To get there, I needed to cross the sports field, and at this time of the day, it was swarming with sports humans.

I needed strategies.

Today I would use the 'the ground is super interesting' approach. That combined with the emergency 'I was just thinking about something' line would keep me from most social situations.

I started the march.

The first leg along the side of the field was clear. Good, no sideline supporters today. I made it passed unchallenged.

The second leg would be more difficult. A small group of randoms was hanging out in the stands. They looked to be all boys.

I focused on my breathing and on the ground, and fast-walked passed them.

There was a whistle.

They are probably not whistling at you, Alex. Keep on walking.

"Hey!" called a voice.

I was almost there. I didn't look up.

"Where are you going?"

I looked over my shoulder and then back to the ground, immediately regretting the move.

"You deaf?" shouted another boy as I cleared the area. He sounded threatening.

My pace quickened. It wasn't far now. My heart was beating fast.

By the time I reached the bank, the boys seemed to have lost interest. I looked back to see if I was followed. No sign of anyone.

At last, I was able to return to my book and join my friends in the other world. I breathed a sigh of relief.

It was so quiet in the sanctuary. The students messing around at school were just a distant murmur. The odor of damp earth and pine needles hung in the air. There were a few birds there, singing to one another.

I sat down, leaning against a tree.

A thrush burrowed its face into the fallen leaves in search of lunch.

I closed my eyes. It was peaceful.

"What are you doing here?" boomed a voice.

CHAPTER 5

I would have jumped if I wasn't sitting down. My eyes raced up and saw Mr. Wilson, the gym teacher. He looked stern. I put my book away, embarrassed.

"What did you put in your bag?" asked Mr. Davis, who was coming at me from the other side. They had cornered me.

"It's a book," I said, slowly taking it out again.

"Were you smoking drugs?" demanded Mr. Wilson.

"No," I said, dumbfounded. The teachers were kind of out of breath.

Was this a bust?

"This area is out of bounds," barked Mr. Davis.

"I was just reading," I said. I was kind of scared. These two grown men were bellowing at me.

"Harry Potter," said Mr. Wilson, cocking his head to read the cover. "Aren't you a little old to be reading Harry Potter?"

Mr. Wilson only had a limited understanding of pop culture. He only had a limited understanding of any culture, for that matter.

"No?" I said, hesitating. "It's my Mom's book."

"Oh," said Mr. Wilson abruptly. "Well, you shouldn't

be here."

"And if we see you here again, it will be detention," said Mr. Davis.

"OK," I squeaked.

I got to my feet and brushed the leaves from my skirt. I was acutely aware of their eyes on me. I started off towards the field, cringing as I thought about walking by those boys again. I'd have to be more careful and hide behind a tree next time.

"Stay away from drugs!" shouted Mr. Wilson as I left.

***

It had been a rough day, and I didn't want to go straight home in case Mom started talking to me about calling Uncle Jack. That was the last thing I needed. I decided instead to go to the shops by the park again and see if I could find the bookshop.

Once I was out of the school grounds, I took out the business card and examined it again. I reread the opening hours aloud to myself, "Spring Showers and Summer Snowstorms."

I examined the sky. It seemed cloudy enough, but would it rain? I could only hope.

Lilly text me to see what had happened to me at lunch. I felt pretty stink about ditching her. I don't know why she hangs out with me.

Looking for a bookshop. Talk later.

As I walked, a chill wind whipped about me. I shivered, pulled my hands inside the sleeves of my oversized maroon sweater, and quickened my pace.

A raindrop fell. I smiled to think that I was pleased to get caught in this weather. Soon the rain was loud as it fell all about me, seeping through my sweater and into my skin. I hurried on towards the shops.

As I approached, I scanned the scene for the bookshop. To my relief, I saw it. There it was, casually real, right between the post office and the grocers. A warm yellow light glowed from within.

I pulled the heavy door open and closed it behind me. The sound of the rain was muted, and I became conscious that I was dripping onto the carpet.

"We are closing in ten minutes," said the scruffy man behind the counter without looking up from his phone. He didn't seem like someone who would own a disappearing shop. Come to think of it, I wasn't sure what such a person should look like. A wizard, maybe?

I love old bookshops, the kind where you feel like you could get lost in the shelves forever, the ones where rows and rows of old books twist and turn impossibly, gaining in mystery the deeper you dare to go. In these shrines, every volume contains an adventure, silently waiting on a dusty shelf. Those are the bookshops I dream of.

This was not that kind of bookshop.

This place looked like it had been stocked by a passing tornado and shelved by an angry pigeon.

I tried to get my bearings. I looked for anything which might point me in the direction of the classics section. I was a sci-fi and fantasy girl at heart, but whenever I was in a new bookshop, I bee-lined straight for the classics. I'm not sure why.

Many of the books were in cardboard boxes, and several of these were stacked on top of each other. My heart boggled to imagine what might be hidden away under all the dust.

Near the back of the store, there was a shelf that was at least partially organized. I skimmed through, but nothing caught my eye. There was a ladder to the uppermost shelves, which I dared not to climb.

A black Labrador poked its head out from under a table. I could hear its tail thudding against something as it wagged somewhere out of sight.

"Hello there," I said.

The dog said nothing.

I patted its head. "Good boy."

The dog had one of those faces where it seemed to be perpetually smiling. I smiled back and returned to my search.

I know what my mother would have said at a time like this. 'Why don't you just ask the guy at the front? It's his job to help you.' People were always saying 'useful' things like that. Oh yeah, I'll just march on up to him and say 'excuse me, where is the classics section?' and pretend that my private universe of Hank was not freaking out.

There was enough freaking out going on just being in the bookshop on my own. I was closer to giving up and leaving the shop altogether than I was to saying two words to the guy behind the counter.

As I scanned the shelves, a familiar name caught my eye: Dickens.

I walked to the shelf and inspected his neighbors: Jane Austen, Charlotte Brontë, and Bram Stoker. He was in good company. I glided my eyes over the ancient spines in search of the same name I always looked for: Lewis Carroll.

"I'm closing up in five," the guy called from the front. I couldn't see him and thought it would be more awkward to be still inside the shop when he closed up than it would be to reply.

"K," I said, and felt bold for doing so.

Then I saw it: Lewis Carroll's Alice's Adventures in Wonderland. It was my favorite book.

I pulled the book from the shelf. It was a beautiful old edition, red with gold leaf. It was the kind of book you dream about when imagining your future home library. I had seen copies like this before. Those copies always seemed to be in high places and behind counters where you couldn't get a closer look without talking to someone first.

The book seemed to be in excellent condition. I leafed through the gorgeous and fragrant pages. I saw all the familiar characters who had kept me company one winter a couple of years ago.

It was an old book, to be sure. I started to wonder how old. I flipped to the front and tried to find the publishing date.

1865.

"Whoa," I said. I held the book with even more reverence. I didn't really know when Alice was first published, but I was fairly sure that this must have been pretty close. I checked the inside cover to see if there was a price on the book. If there were no price, then there would be no sale, in accordance with a well-established rule for people like me.

$1.99

"I'm closing up!"

My heart was pounding. I had to have this book!

But then something dreadful occurred to me. I didn't have any money in my checking account! I always transferred everything over to my savings. If I were going to be able to buy this book today, I would have to transfer some money. Now.

I opened my banking app with shaking fingers. The loading screen seemed to take forever.

No Internet.

I waved my arm around in the air, but the screen did not load. Then I remembered the ladder. I looked back to the front of the shop. There was no movement. It was now or never. I climbed up the first few steps of the ladder. No signal. I climbed a couple more.

"I'm serious," said the man.

"Just a second," I called.

The dog watched me with curious eyes.

There it was! A single bar of signal. The app loaded. I selected $20 to transfer, just in case they wanted to charge me more for some reason. I was always worried about that sort of thing.

I didn't have time to check that it had gone through. If I didn't get to the front of the store now then maybe the man wouldn't sell the book to me. Someone else would find it, and I would miss out.

Or the store would disappear.

I walked to the front of the store, trying to look casual and placed the book on the counter. "Just that, thanks," I said. It was the only thing I ever said to shop-people. It was slightly less awkward than saying nothing at all.

"$1.99," he said without checking the price. I handed him my card. He took it and placed it on the paywave scanner right in front of me.

My body was alive with the feelings of awkward.

There must be a dimension of time that opens up especially for moments like this.

Did the money go through, or not?

I always assumed that shop people thought I might be trying to steal from them, or that they thought I was trying to pay with no money. I don't know why I thought this, but it usually contributes to me feeling, and probably appearing, highly conspicuous.

This was by far the worst moment. ACCEPTED or DECLINED? Random numbers and connections that I didn't understand would decide.

I held my breath.

CHAPTER 6

The man handed me my card, receipt, and the book. "Thanks," I stammered and fled out of the store and into the rain. I tucked the precious book inside my sweater and under my arm and started to run.

"You're late back," said Mom, the instant I was in the door. Ordinarily, this would cause me to tense up, but I was far too excited.

"I found a bookshop. Have a look," I handed Mom my new treasure.

She turned down the stovetop and sat down to examine my find. I felt like a cat that had killed a bird for its master. I kind of wish cats brought you books. That would be pretty much the best thing.

"Alice's Adventures in Wonderland," she read aloud, "don't you already have a copy?"

"Look at the date at the front."

"1865. That's pretty old. Victorian. How much did you pay for it?"

"Only two dollars," I said, smiling like an idiot. "I think it might be a first edition."

Mom's face went kind of blank. "First edition? Are you sure?"

"I think so."

"First editions of major nineteenth-century writers sell at auction for millions of dollars, Alex." Her tone was stern. Angry?

My heart sank. For a dreadful moment, I thought that Mom was going to make me take it back to the store.

"Really?" I said, feeling afraid.

"Where did you say you got it?"

"The bookshop down the road. Between the post office and the veggie shop."

"Huh," said Mom, distant now.

Mom was quite introspective at dinner, which kind of made everyone quiet, everyone but Dad. He was kind of on a different wavelength from the rest of us.

"Why is everyone not talking? Did someone die?" he asked, grinning. I imagined what he would say if someone actually had died, and he was smiling about it.

I decided that I would not learn the books first edition status until I had read it through at least once.

I wanted to make sure I had the perfect reading environment. I tended to read no matter what the circumstances: bus, family gatherings, the beach. When I was little, I used to read books in the car at night, one sentence at a time by catching the light from each passing street lamp. But just because I don't need specific conditions for reading doesn't mean I don't appreciate them.

I began by giving my room a bit of a clean. By clean, I mean I stuffed things under my bed and inside my closet. I put my school things out of sight to give myself the illusion that they didn't exist.

I cleared a space on my desk and lit the candle which Grandma gave me for Christmas. It was small, lavender scented, and precious.

"Alex!" called Mom.

I closed my eyes in frustration. "Yeah?"

"Can you come and help Jonny with his homework?"

"Mom! I'm busy!"

"I don't ask much of you, Alex," she was walking up the stairs now. That's how I could tell I was going to lose.

The scent of the candle caught in my nose. I decided not to blow it out. Instead, I let the aroma fill the room in my absence.

Jonny was at the kitchen table. He was drawing bees on his math homework. "Do you think they sing songs when they are sad?" asked Jonny as I sat down.

"Who?"

"The bees that live near the swings in the park."

"I don't know, Jonny," I said.

"I hope they are OK."

It was a real struggle to get his attention back to multiplication. After about half an hour, we still weren't done, but we were done enough. I loved Jonny, but Mom had trained him just to wait for me or her to show him the answers. It was enormously frustrating.

Now it was time for tea. Once the kettle was boiled, I poured the hot water into my largest ornate teacup. The water collided with the English Breakfast tea bag, and aromatic steam swirled upward. I smiled.

I took a quick shower while the tea brewed. Once back in my room, I pulled on my Tardis pajamas, took a sip of my tea, and lay out on my bed. My hair was still wet and smelled of shampoo.

I carefully read the cover of the book. Most of the books I owned had tacky, poorly designed covers, the sort that gave rise to much-repeated phrases. This book was different. It was a truly beautiful object. Within a simple golden circle against a red background was Alice, looking out at me, waiting for me to join her.

I didn't much care if this book was worth millions of dollars. It was to be the prize of my collection, and I bought it for pretty much nothing.

I opened the book to the first page and was greeted by that familiar fragrant smell that only truly old books acquired. It mingled with the lavender scent from the candle beautifully. I breathed it in and began to read.

Alice was beginning to get very tired...

I never finished that sentence.

The light in my peripheral darkened. At first, I thought it was the candle flickering and going out. I felt like I was going to faint.

My heart stopped beating. What's happening? I mouthed. I was scared, or at least I think I was scared. Fear is a weird concept when you don't have a heartbeat.

Then I was falling.

It was like the page of the book was rushing at me. Soon it filled my entire experience, and I completely lost awareness of my body. All around me, I could hear a rustling sound like paper caught in the wind. This was no ordinary wind. It circled me, carrying with it the sweet smell of ancient books and rainy days.

I tried to call out, but there was no air in my lungs. I thought I was dying and found myself feeling guilty for not texting Lilly first.

Time lost its meaning.

My world drained away completely. From my room, the center of comfort in the universe, to utter darkness, chaos, and confusion.

CHAPTER 7

When I opened my eyes, all I could see was a groove between two burgundy tiles, one of which was smushed into my face. It was cold against my cheek. I felt like I had woken up after an afternoon nap, disoriented and confused. I tried to remember where I had fallen asleep, but my memory was hazy.

I got to my feet, straightened out my pajamas, and looked around. The first thing I realized was that I was in a public place. The second thing I realized was that I was in a library.

But this was like no library I had ever seen before.

It was a mosaic of staircases, ladders, and shelves, rising through level after level. My eyes followed upward until I was looking at what really ought to have been the ceiling but was, in fact, more library.

I wandered.

There were no sounds in the library save for my own footfall. There was no one anywhere to be seen. I was completely alone. Worries about walking around in my pajamas began to subside as I walked.

In no time at all, I was lost and in the most wonderful

way.

This library was the sort that lingers on the edge of the imagination but is never quite realized. It was more than just a collection of books, it was an ornate temple to reading. Almost every surface that could be polished hardwood was polished hardwood. The paths twisted and turned. The rich smell of old books occasionally mingled with some flowering vine curling down a staircase rail or a row of dried flowers hanging from above.

In this place, one could learn the true meaning of nook. Every conceivable variety of chair, day-bed, and floor bag was arranged in every conceivable way. From under staircases and amongst the shelves, to hanging from thick ropes, swaying gently.

Whenever I came to a window, and there were many, I looked out, but what I saw never made any sense. Some of the windows looked out over sea cliffs and distant rain, others over deep valleys and rolling fog. Others looked over sun-drenched gardens, the sound of bees humming from somewhere among the petals and pollen.

My heart swelled with awe and wonder. How could this place exist? How could it really be? It was like someone had reached into my dreams and recreated the ultimate place of comfort and exploration.

I came upon an open space fitted with large glass cases where maps were displayed. I wandered silently among them. Now and then, a coast or mountain range caught my eye, and I was drawn into the map, tracing its lines and reading the strange names of distant places.

Time lost all meaning in the library.

I felt my legs ache from wandering but couldn't say how far I had strayed. A distant and familiar sound caught my attention. It was the unmistakable sound of a kettle ready to boil. I made my way towards that sound.

The kettle clicked as I rounded a corner, but it was nowhere to be seen. Instead, there was a large teapot and a set of little teacups arranged on a side table.

I poured myself a cup and looked about for somewhere to sit. A sizeable green couch caught my eye. It was under a window that hung in the air on the end of two long chains.

I walked around the window. On each side, there seemed to be a different scene. On one side, there was a lake on a fine day. On the other, there was a green countryside drenched in rain. I curled up and sipped my tea.

"Is someone there?" asked a voice.

I sat up and looked around. I couldn't see anyone. The voice was thickly accented, Scottish like Professor McGonagall's.

Hank heard it too. He clawed at my innards and reminded me that I was in my pajamas.

Feeling the urge to hide, I stood up from my seat, crouched behind the nearest shelf, and froze.

I could hear that someone was getting closer. There was something strange about the sound they made as they walked. I looked at the teacup I was still holding. Did I steal someone's tea? Was I even supposed to be here?

They were getting closer now. Soon, they would find me hiding as conspicuously as possible. I looked about for somewhere to go. I saw a flight of stairs and crept towards it, trying to be as quiet as I possibly could.

"I saw you there," called the voice.

I cringed as each step made the stairs creak. When I reached the top, I chose a direction at random and hurried as fast as I could. There was the thud-thud of movement behind me, but I dared not turn around.

My heart was racing now.

I ducked down another row of books and began to run. Candles set in lamps of brass and gold spontaneously lit as I approached them, spaced as they were, every eight steps.

I saw a door, old and imposing. I grabbed the handle, pulled it open, and plunged forward into the darkness.

All was silent but for my beating heart. I tried to catch my breath.

There was a vague smell of old fabric. I shuffled forward best I could and collided with a hanging curtain. My eyes started to adjust.

In the gray light, I could see the vague silhouette of a huge piano a few feet ahead of me. Slowly, I walked forward, captivated by its imposing shape. When I was close, I reached out and softly pressed one of the great keys.

Light suddenly filled the room as three magnificent chandeliers lit.

I was standing on a stage and looking out at an empty auditorium. My attention was once more drawn to the fact that I was in my pajamas. This was the stuff of nightmares. Hank burrowed deep into my gut and started pulling on things.

"I can see you, you know," said the voice, "wait there, would you?"

I ran across the stage, into the wing, and through another door. It opened out onto a great cliff. I almost ran right off the edge, but stopped just in time, swaying on the precipice.

It was an enormous canyon, lined on both sides with rows and rows of books.

I was still in the library.

I scanned the scene for some way out. There was a ladder leading up to the top of the canyon. I made for it. It was wooden and old and felt like it might collapse under my weight.

I heard the door below me open, and I briefly glanced back. A hulking great shape was down there. What on earth was chasing me?

I ran down another row of books, and then another, searching for an escape. I saw a double door, wooden and ornate. Pushing my way through, I was soon in another dark room.

This room was circular in shape. A pale silvery light hung over several desks and shelves which were stacked with thick volumes. I looked up and saw that the ceiling was a glass dome.

The light was coming from the stars.

My wonder was broken by the sound of the door opening behind me. I looked about for someplace to run, someplace to hide, but there were no more exits.

I was trapped.

The hulking shadow thudded closer and closer.

There was nothing I could do but stand there and wait, wait with a beating heart.

CHAPTER 8

There you are," it said. Its massive eyes were foil in the starlight.

There I was, face to face with an eight-foot gorilla. Its face took up most of my field of vision, illuminated by the same soft blue glow that hung over everything else.

It was wearing spectacles.

The scene was more than I could comprehend. Overwhelmed and exhausted, I collapsed where I stood.

When I awoke, I was lying on an exceedingly comfortable couch. An empty silence hung in the air, cleaved only by a faint tick-tock coming from somewhere out of sight. Looking about, I could see that I was still in the library, in some kind of reading room.

For a moment, I wanted to believe that what I had seen was some dream. My mind was hazy, and maybe it could have been a dream, but for the gorilla pouring me tea.

"Oh, good, you are awake. Easy now," said the gorilla.

I had never seen any animal so massive before. It moved with a grace that seemed unnatural for its size.

"You have had a nasty shock, I think."

"Where am I?" I asked, sitting up.

"You are in The Library, dear. Here have a cuppa. This

will do you a world of good."

She handed me the most beautiful ornate teacup, pinched delicately between a giant forefinger and thumb. It certainly looked like regular tea.

I took a sip.

"I don't remember going to a library," I said.

"Yes, well, I was afraid of that. But I have to tell you, this isn't just any old library, miss. This is *The* Library."

"*The* Library?"

"Rest your head, dear. I'll fill you in when you have finished your tea."

With care, the gorilla walked out of the room, knuckles to the ground, swaying gently.

Though it all seemed like madness, I felt calm. The gorilla had a manner that put me at ease, strange as it seemed.

Some ten minutes later, the gorilla returned and sat down beside me, placing one enormous hand on my shoulder.

"How are you feeling, dear? I know it can be a bit of a shock coming to a place like this. You let me know when you are ready for me to show you around. Not everywhere, of course, but the important places."

"I think that I am ready now," I said, though I was not at all certain that this was true.

"Great. Well then, if you would just follow me."

My body was reluctant, but I forced myself to my feet.

"Who are you?" I asked as I followed the gorilla out the door.

"Well, I am the Librarian, of course. And how would you like to be addressed?"

"My name is Alexandria," I said, "just Alex is fine."

The Librarian gave me a sideways glance, "I think I'll stick with Alex," she said.

She led me through the shelves of books, weaving between them on a seemingly random path.

"Forgive me for saying," I said haltingly, "but you are a gorilla, right?"

"Yes."

"How does a gorilla wind up as a librarian?"

"I have a lot of experience running libraries," she said defensively.

"I see."

"You will find that The Library holds many mysteries, especially for outsiders. You could wander these shelves forever and still not uncover all there is to know."

"Where is this place?"

"Where? That is not a question that greatly fits The Library. The Library is where it is. There is nothing else."

"I don't understand."

"Well, you come from a place, and this place is next to that place."

"Torbay?"

"No, I don't think so. Next to your entire world. I have to admit, I don't know much about where you are from. We don't get a lot of visitors here, and there are so many books."

"There must be every book that has ever been written."

"Yes, and every book that ever will be written too. These books are not just books as you understand them from your own world. They contain within them the lives of every creature in every universe from the smallest tardigrade to the most massive space-whale. These books are constantly writing themselves, filling their pages."

"Writing themselves?"

"Yes. Autobiographies, you might say."

"What is the purpose of having so many books about people's lives? Do people read them?"

"It's not that these books are about people's lives, these books *are* people's lives. They are very precious, that is why The Library needs a Keeper. If anything were to happen to these books, then it would not just affect the lives of that individual but the entire world they inhabit. And this stretches across time and space, generation to generation. They are very precious books."

"And are you the Keeper?"

"No, no. I am the Librarian. I already told you that. We recently lost our Keeper and are in the process of training the new one."

"Are you taking me to them now?"

"In a manner of speaking."

We came to the great canyon. The Librarian led me across a stone bridge. I looked out over the expanse. There seemed to be clouds some distance below.

"Be careful around these books," said the Librarian as we crossed, "they are a bit edgy."

"Edgy?"

The Librarian laughed, deep and rich. "Just my little joke. It's actually where we keep the cliffhangers."

After a time we came to the place where I had seen all the maps. The Librarian scanned the cabinets, searching for something.

"We will start with someplace familiar."

Carefully she pulled out a map and handed it to me. I read the description. "Paris?"

"This is in your world, isn't it?"

"Yes."

"Have you ever been to Paris?"

"No, have you?" I imagined for a moment an eight-foot gorilla sitting at a small café sipping a latte.

"I have never been to your world. I must admit I am curious about this Paris."

"Oh," I said, not quite catching what she meant.

"Let's go!"

Before I could say anything, she took my hand and touched it to the map.

Quite suddenly, the world began to spin.

The books and bookshelves, cabinets and maps, candles and chairs, all of them spun around me. I felt my heart stop, and the air drain from my lungs. It was happening again.

My memory was coming back, and I was starting to remember how I came to be in The Library. I had been reading my new book.

Now where was I going?

The next breath I breathed was the cold night air. I looked about the scene. We were on top of a tall building set in a sprawling cityscape. "Are we in Paris?" I asked.

"You tell me," said the Librarian, "I've never been here, remember?"

The sounds of traffic hummed all around us, punctuated occasionally by the beep of a horn.

"Neither have I," I said, searching for the Eiffel Tower.

"Well, I can say that unless our maps are completely off, which they most certainly are not, then we are definitely in Paris."

"How can you be sure?"

"Because in a very real sense our maps *are* Paris. Shall we take a look around?"

"Um, I don't know how to tell you this, but in my world, it is not very common for, that is to say, people like you. Gorillas–"

"You don't have gorillas here?"

"Well, we do, but they're not very common in places like Paris."

"I don't mind a bit of attention."

"Do you mind getting captured and put in a cage?"

The Librarian was silent for a moment.

"Why don't we go somewhere else?" she suggested.

She pointed to the map that I was holding. It was no longer a map of Paris but had become a map of The Library. It was constantly shifting and changing.

"How did I get this?"

"It came with you, of course. How else do you think we go back?"

She touched my hand to it, and we began to fall in. Within moments we had landed back in The Library. Soon the Librarian was looking around for a different map.

"Sydney? What about Sydney?"

"Same deal, I'm afraid."

"Oh, dear. I've been curious about these maps for some

time. The Library never had a Keeper from your world before. I guess I won't get as much exploring done there as I had hoped."

"I'm sorry."

She turned and looked at me with her watery black eyes. They were enormous. "You don't think less of me for being a gorilla, do you? I mean, you're not feeling any urges to lock me up or anything?"

"No. Of course not," I said. "I'm fine with you being a gorilla. I mean, why not?"

The Librarian smiled, "that's nice of you to say."

I smiled and shrugged. Comforting a giant Scottish gorilla woman was the strangest situation I had ever been in.

"How is all this possible?"

"You see, Alex. Keepers have certain privileges when it comes to The Library."

"I don't understand. I thought we were going to meet the Keeper?"

The Librarian leaned in close, her giant face inches from my own, and whispered. "Well, that's the thing, Alex. When I said we have a new Keeper in training, I was talking about you."

CHAPTER 9

Me?" I asked, taking a step back.

"Yes, you. You have been selected," said the Librarian.

"There must be some mistake," I wanted to tell her that I wasn't the Keeper, couldn't be the Keeper. I wanted to tell her that I was just Alex.

"No mistake, I know a Keeper when I see one."

"What if I am no good? I don't have any experience running a library."

"Good thing for you that running The Library is my job. It is your job to keep it safe. Don't you worry. I'll teach you everything that you need to know."

"Teach me? Is there going to be an exam?"

"No exam, no, but there's a good deal to learn. It is a sacred responsibility to be a Keeper, to look after all these books. It is more than just sitting about in The Library's many lounges reading books all day. Though I'm pleased to say that that does take up a large proportion of the job."

"OK, that doesn't sound so bad."

"Sometimes, it can be tough, though. The books will call to you, Alex. It is vitally important that you listen closely and respond to that call, no matter how hard it might be."

"They will call to me?"

"You see, Alex, sometimes books get in trouble. It doesn't happen all the time, but it does happen. And when it does, it will be your job to help them out."

"Help them out?"

"To dive deep into the stories, and do what needs to be done."

"How will I know what needs to be done?"

"You will learn that with time. Follow your instincts, and you won't go too far wrong."

"What is the call like?"

"Sometimes you will be here walking about, sitting, or reading, and you will see a book, and you'll just get a feeling. You will feel a pull, an urge to pick it up, to open it up, and to start reading. It is vitally important that you pay attention to this feeling."

"What if I miss it?"

"Most people know when it is time to read. You will be no different," she smiled kindly. "Well, Alex, it is getting late in your world, and it is probably time for you to go home and get some rest. I will have a lot to teach you tomorrow, so make sure you hurry back."

"Um, I have school tomorrow. I wish I could hurry back, but I can't come back until after school."

"Ah, yes. The education of young people. Very important. Well, make sure that you drop in when you are finished with your classes for the day."

"Of course!"

"I can tell that The Library is going to be lucky to have you."

"Thank you, Librarian. Um, just one thing. How do I go home? And how do I come back again?"

"Well, you use your key. There is always a key. Do you have it?"

"I don't know what you mean. What key?"

"It will be a book, or a map, something made of paper usually. What were you looking at before you came to The Library?"

"Oh, I got this new book from a bookshop that is only open in the spring rains and the summer snowstorms."

"That place is still open? Yes, well, that would be the book."

I withdrew my copy of Alice's Adventures in Wonderland from my bag and held it up.

"How did it get in my bag? How did I know it would be in my bag?"

"Library magic," said the Librarian.

"How do I use it?"

"All you need to do is open to the first chapter and start reading. You will find that most things worth doing in life begin with the opening chapter of a book. As you become more attached to a book, the book will become more attached to you. It will never be hard to find the books you need in The Library. They are almost always right nearby."

"I like that," I said, grinning at the gorilla, "I'll see you tomorrow then."

The Librarian nodded.

I flipped the book open and began to read.

***

As I walked to school, my mind spun with all that had happened the previous night. I had a whole library inside one little book. *The* Library, as the Librarian called it. Everything I thought I knew about the world had been turned on its head. Was it magic? Or was there some strange science at work? All I knew was that the world was a much more peculiar place than I had previously thought.

Lilly and I had this thing where whoever got to school first would wait at the front gate for the other so we could walk in together. Sometimes this meant that we were very late for class, but that was OK. We didn't like to break with tradition.

On that morning, Lilly got there first. She was absorbed by her phone. I debated within myself whether to tell Lilly about The Library.

She looked up as I approached, and her usual silly smile erupted over her face. "Did you know that if you are burned alive, you only feel it until your nerve endings are destroyed?"

"Hi, Lilly. Who are you burning?"

"No one at present. I was going to do my speech on the persecution of witches, but I'm finding the topic of immolation way more interesting."

I really wanted to know that I wasn't crazy. If I could just get Lilly to see The Library, then at least I would know that I could trust my own mind.

"What spooked you, Alex? You look spooked."

"No, I'm fine."

"Good, because I ain't got no time for no spooked

friend."

I grew anxious. What if Lilly thought I was a loon? She was my only friend. I looked at my watch, it was only a couple of moments before the bell would ring for class.

"Hey, Lilly, I have a question."

"Shoot."

"Has anything weird ever happened to you?"

"I find all of existence weird. It's so mundane, which frankly I think is a bit suspicious."

"Come on."

"Weird as when my identical Danish twin was in that toothpaste commercial?"

I hesitated. Lilly was Lilly. Would she even understand?

"Gnorts, Alex. You are killing me. What are you on about?"

Right, I was just going to go ahead and say it. "Do you believe in magic?"

"I swear miss, those are just mathematical formulas and scientific instruments," she said in a fairly convincing southern accent, "I ain't never spoken to the devil. He never returns my calls. If you see him, you go and tell him that banana is a suitable binding agent in the construction of muffins."

"Never mind."

"Sorry, not sure where that came from. Maybe I was possessed?!"

The bell rang.

CHAPTER 10

At lunchtime, I was ambushed by Lilly, armed with her mobile phone. She snapped a photo of me before I could say anything.

"No, that's no good."

"Thanks."

"Just back up a bit, I want to take another one."

"You know how I feel about photographs. I don't want any evidence of my existence. Why are you trying to steal my soul, Lilly?"

"It's for your Instagram account."

"Figures. I don't want my face all over the Internet, Lilly. It's weird."

"It's just for your profile."

"My profile?"

"It's for your drawings."

"What drawings?"

"Your dragons, you spoon. Unless you have other drawings?"

"No, not really. I don't know, Lilly. I'm not sure if I want to share them."

"It is fortunate for you then that I am sure that I want you to share them. Do you have any on your phone?"

I pulled out my phone and accessed my gallery. It was a collection of all my best. I liked to scroll through them occasionally to remind myself that at least there was one thing that I could do well. Most of them were drawn on my tablet, but some of them were the pencil sketches I scanned. Gingerly I handed my phone to Lilly.

"Oh, wow, these are good."

"Yeah?" It felt nice hearing someone say that. It was like I was being told I had permission to exist or something. I know it's weird, but when you don't think much of yourself, it sort of feels like you need that kind of permission.

"I mean, like, actually good. Wow, you sure like dragons. This one is my favorite. No, this one is."

She handed the phone back to me. Looking back at me was a dragon I had drawn a couple of weeks back. It was holding a buttercup and looked like it had been looking at the flower before noticing I was there. It was my favorite too.

"We are not gonna put them up all at once, we have to create a strategy, like, once a week or something."

"Hey, hang on. I don't know if I want my drawings on the Internet."

"I thought we already covered this. These dragons are excellent. It would be cruelty to deny them freedom. They want to be free, Alex. What kind of monster are you?"

"A serious one."

"You will need a new account, though. Dragongirl is probably already taken. I suppose we could put numbers on the end?" she was tapping away at her phone now, engrossed in something.

"Aflowerfromyourdragon," said Lilly, holding up her phone.

"Doesn't look like a flower."

"No, I mean the name. It's available on Instagram, Facebook, and Tumblr. It's too long for Youtube, but I know how you feel about video, so that won't be a problem."

"Wait, what's happening?"

"I guess it is kind of long," said Lilly.

I liked the idea of sharing some of my work, but I know how it would turn out. I'd post my favorite, and it would get a whole lot of likes and comments, and I'd feel fantastic. Dad would probably comment on it with something awkward, demonstrating once again that he wasn't clear on what the difference was between a comment and a private message.

That would be super cringe.

Then I'd post another and people will say nice things, but it won't be as much, and I'd feel terrible. Then I'd keep on posting, chasing the dragon, so to speak.

But eventually, I'll be exposed as not having proper talent. People would like my posts because they feel like they have to, like their daily Alex chore or something, and I will have successfully found another way to be an inconvenience on everyone's lives. No, thank you.

"Velociraptorgirl is taken."

"I don't really draw dinosaurs."

"What? No, I mean for me. I figure that if I draw a velociraptor every day for a year, then eventually, I'll get really good. Then whenever anyone needs a drawing of a velociraptor, I'll be their man. Could maybe branch out into other theropods, but only once I've established myself as an authority."

"You do that, Lilly."

**

That afternoon I wasted no time in getting home and back to my book. I closed my bedroom door and pulled out Alice and started to read. Just like the previous night, I began to fall. All the same, things happened. My heart stopped, my lungs drained, and I was pulled into the pages. However, this time, it was less distressing. I was going to The Library, and that was awesome.

When I landed, I saw the Librarian walking down a row of shelves. She was carrying a stack of books.

"Hello," I said.

"Hello there, Alex! Good that you are here. Help me with these, would you?"

I took the top book from her pile and went to tuck it under an arm when the title of the book caught my eye.

Darcy Knight

"I know him," I said.

"Do you now?"

"He goes to my school."

"I'm sorry to hear that."

"How come?"

"Because his story has been touched, Alex."

"What do you mean?"

"It has been tainted by the void of creation. Let me show you."

She placed her stack of books on the floor where she was standing and led me on. As we walked, I noticed that the light was changing. Most of the main area of The Library was lit by warm candles and some other more mysterious luminescence.

But as we walked, the light shifted from orange to blue. It grew brighter and with more and more intensity. At last, we came to an open space. In the center of the space was what looked like a miniature blue sun.

Lightning crackled over its surface. The sphere hovered some distance above a stone base. It was roughly the size of an elephant and was completely out of place in The Library.

"What is it?"

"Tell me, Alex, how much do you know about the creation of the universe?"

"Um, not a lot. I know that there was a big bang."

"Ah yes, the big bang. From an infinitely small point outside of space and time, massively condensed matter began to expand rapidly. Now, when you picture that tiny speck of everything, can you tell me where it is?"

"I don't know."

"When you picture it?"

"When I picture it, I see it in darkness with nothing else around, but that's not right, is it?"

"No, it isn't! Because how could there be something outside of that condensed speck of matter if everything that exists is condensed within it?"

"I guess that it is just impossible for us to picture it, maybe?"

"Yes. That is exactly it. You see, the universe started from a speck within the great void. The void is, in essence, lacking in essence. It is nothingness itself. It is the great canvas. The thing on which all is painted. It is the source of all creation and creative energy. When harnessed, it can do amazing things."

"It is weird to think about."

"It is impossible to think about. It can be fun to try, but we shouldn't delude ourselves into thinking that we can ever get close to getting close."

"What does all that have to do with this?" I gestured towards the miniature sun.

"What we see in front of us is the Heart of The Library. It is a piece of the void. In the same way that the books both are and are not the people within them, this orb both is and is not that ancient void, that primordial creative nothingness."

"I thought you just said that it was impossible for us to even get close to thinking about it?"

"It is, that is why we have the Heart of The Library. It helps. Now, your friend there, his story has been touched by the void. There have been some instances when this has not led to disaster, but such instances are rare."

"Is he in trouble?"

"Terrible trouble, I'm afraid. He has been for some time. You see, those who have been touched by the void must suffer the forces of chaos and magic entering into their lives. It will likely claim him in the end."

"Oh," I said. My mind drifted back to the sword Darcy had at school. Maybe he needed to be armed?

"The Library and its Heart are one. They are mirror images that just happen to look very different. It is both the most powerful and the most dangerous thing that there is. As The Library's Keeper, you must make sure that the power of the void does not fall into the wrong hands."

"How can I possibly do that? That's far too much for me to handle!" I protested.

"I have been running The Library for some time, Alex. One thing that I know with absolute certainty is that character is far more important than someone's age, experience, or skill set. Give yourself some time to adjust. There are forces in the multiverse that work tirelessly, day and night, trying to seize the power of the void. Dark forces. I don't want to hide that from you. But you will learn to handle them and defeat them. Just give yourself time."

I looked at her, doubting.

"Come, let me show you something."

After a brief hike through rows of shelves, we came to a familiar set of ornate double doors. It was where I had tried to hide from the Librarian only the day before. She led me inside.

I walked into the darkness and blinked. In the soft starlight, I could make out dark shapes swirling about the room. Every so often, they collided into one another with a crash.

"Oh, shoot," said the Librarian. She grabbed a broom from against the wall and started to hit at the objects.

"What is it?"

"Accretion."

"Sorry?"

"They are trying to form planets. It is very irritating. You see, this is what they did to come into being in the first place. Planetary formation is a hard habit to break."

"The books are planets?"

"No, but they contain planets. In a manner of speaking."

The Librarian gave up with the broom. She climbed up one of the shelving ladders and jumped at the largest clump of books. They crashed to the floor with a thud and a clap. The remaining books began to slow. The Librarian took up her broom again and easily knocked them from their orbits.

"There, that's better," she said, catching her breath.

"Is that a common occurrence?"

"That entirely depends on prevailing philosophical discourse. I wish they would just settle on a theory and be done with it."

"Right," I said, understanding only in part.

"You will find that it is always a clear and starry night in here."

"They are beautiful," I said, staring upwards at the millions of twinkling lights.

"Pick one."

"Pick one?"

"Yes, pick one. Point to one. Any one. It doesn't matter."

I did as she asked and pointed at a star.

"Ah, no. Pick a different one. Sorry."

I chose a different star.

"An excellent choice. Wait there."

The Librarian began scanning the shelves, shaking her head, pulling books out, putting them back, and scratching her chin. "Ah-ha," she said, at last. The Librarian picked up a volume from the floor. She flicked through and handed it to me with a page open.

I took the giant book in my arms. It was heavy. In the low light, I could just make out a drawing of a star system. Six planets were orbiting a red star.

"You see the second planet from the star? I want you to press it."

"Like this?" I pressed at the planet. The star system faded off the page and turned to a map of a world. It was mostly made up of vast red continents with a few yellowy-green seas.

"This planet sits in what is called the Goldilocks Zone, not too cold, not too hot. Would you like to go there?"

"We can do that?" I asked, deadpan.

"We sure can. Hopefully, it is more hospitable than Paris."

"Okay, tell me what to do."

"Just press where you want to go," she said, smiling.

"Like this?" I pressed in the center of the largest continent.

"No, not there!" cried the Librarian.

We fell.

CHAPTER 11

We landed in a red desert. I looked around. It was all dust for as far as I could see.

"That was close," said the Librarian.

"Did I do something wrong?"

"No, well, we almost fell into a lake of sulphuric acid, but no. It's not your fault."

"I don't see it."

"It's quite far off, I think. Map travel can be very inaccurate, you see."

"The light is strange here." It looked like it was the very moment of twilight.

"I think this planet may be tidally locked. It always looks like this here."

"It's beautiful," I said, captivated.

"I am sorry that there is no life about. It is always the life which is the most interesting."

"This place is magical."

"Most planets harbored life at some stage, and still would if it weren't for entropy."

"Entropy?"

"Life takes hold. It evolves. It adapts to new environments. It thrives. And sooner or later, well, there it is."

"There what is?"

She gestured to the surrounding wasteland. "Extinction finds a way."

***

We jumped back to The Library, and I found myself once more in that starry room. The Librarian led me out and down another set of corridors. It seemed to me that we were heading again to the Heart of the Library.

We stopped next to a well-stocked shelf of particularly ornate books.

"Now that I've shown you the maps and the planetary atlases, it is time to show you the stories. This is where all the real action happens."

"Are you telling me we can go into the books?"

"I sure am."

"That's amazing! Why did you wait to tell me that?" My mind was spinning with the possibilities.

"Because it can be dangerous. There is always a lot happening in a book. Always remember, these books are people's lives. Some books will need you to take action to put things right, but just as important is knowing when to leave a story to play itself through."

"OK. I think I'm ready."

"No matter what happens, make sure that you do not bring anything back through with you into The Library, and certainly do not take any person you should meet through."

"How come?"

"Because you risk mixing up different stories. This mustn't be done. It can take forever to sort out down the line. You remove one character, and you would think the plot would hold together, but no. You don't want to be stuck doing book edits for the rest of your life, do you?"

"I suppose not."

The Librarian took down a blue book with ornate gold leaf. A pattern of vines weaved and swirled all over the cover. The title was Elberath.

"It's beautiful," I said.

"It certainly is," said the Librarian, lost in thought. "On this shelf, you will find many books which have survived being touched by the void."

"Survived? How?"

"Due to the careful work of countless Keepers. They all have a bit of chaos still, but are relatively safe these days."

"Where are all the Keepers now?"

The Librarian hesitated. "Mostly they retire back to their own worlds. No one can be expected to curate creation forever. It is tiring work! Now-"

"You said mostly? What about the others?"

"I don't want to worry you, but sometimes they simply disappear. One day they will be here with me, I'll pass them in the halls and smile, and then I'll never see them again."

"Oh."

"The Library needs a Keeper. Sooner or later, it finds a new one. Keepers always turn up with different stories. Sometimes they have inherited a key from an elderly relative. Sometimes they turn up with tales of ghostly figures or disappearing bookshops. There is only ever one Keeper."

"So, what happened to the last Keeper?"

"She went back to her own lands. She was only going to be away for a day or two. That was a while ago now. You remind me of her, actually."

"Thanks."

"I wouldn't worry about such things if I were you. The Keeper probably settled down with her family. She had many friends, as I recall."

Not that much like me then, I thought.

"Now, this book is full of life, not like that empty planet. It is a sort of a vacation spot for me. Lots of jungle and lakes and lovely things like that."

"Is Elberath a person?"

"Yes, or at least he was. If he is still alive now, then he must be ancient. I'll just take you around a quick tour of his kingdom. We won't be bothering him."

She handed me the book. I opened it to the first chapter and began to read.

It was the year 2192 of the second age...

Soon we were falling fast.

We landed on a muddy path in the middle of a dense jungle. All around me was the noise of insects and birds. There were things in the trees too, jumping from here to there. Squirrels maybe?

"Just wonderful, isn't it? I like it here."

"It's lovely."

Just then, a pair of insects sped through the undergrowth and into our path. They looked like wasps but were the size of cats.

"Shoot, I always forget about them," said the Librarian.

"What are they?"

"Run!"

The enormous gorilla bounded off into the trees with a crash. The wasps had seen us and were hurtling towards me. I leaped after the Librarian.

The jungle floor was a mess of vines and logs and streams. Plants with sharp leaves cut at my legs. Stray twigs whipped at my arms.

The wasps were closing in.

The Librarian stopped. "Jump on my back!" she shouted. I did as she asked, just as the wasps were almost upon us.

The Librarian picked up her pace. I held tight as she thudded on. She looked back over her shoulder and then ran even harder.

After a while, she slowed to a stop. She panted as she caught her breath. An assortment of twigs and leaves clung to her black fur. "We," gasp, "lost," gasp, "them."

She set me down on my feet, and I collapsed against a standing stone, sinking to the ground. There were two similar stones nearby, each as tall as I was. They formed a sort of circle around a crop of red mushrooms.

"Well, this is just great," said the Librarian, "we must be miles away now."

"Miles away? From where?"

"I wanted to show you the city here. It is really something special. The market is among the most lively and interesting that I have ever seen, and I have seen a great many."

"I love markets."

"Also, they have no problem with gorillas here, which I suppose I should consider a bonus." She gave me an accusing look.

"It sounds like just the place for us then."

"OK, I have a plan. There is a hill a little while that way," she gestured to what looked like just more jungle. "I'll be able to get a good look from there. Some of these hills have stone seats that make your vision go all funny and show you things a great distance away. Hopefully, it's one of them."

"Sure," I said, ready to stand up.

"No, you wait here. I'll get there quicker that way. If you run into any trouble, just go back to The Library. But make sure you come back for me. I shan't be long."

She crashed into the mess of trees and vines. I listened to her progress for a while. The sounds faded into the distance, and soon I was alone.

I took a moment to consider where I was. The powers of The Library were simply incredible. To all the world, I was shut up in my room reading a book. Yet here I was, in the middle of the most magnificent jungle, sitting among these picturesque stones.

They seemed familiar, somehow.

I searched my memory for the association. Then it struck me. They looked like the circles in the fairy forest back home. The mushrooms completed the association. It felt like I was in a children's book.

I sat and absorbed the nostalgic scene. A ladybug the

size of a mouse crawled across the clearing. I followed her progress over the mud and leaves.

That's when I saw them. Two figures walked into the clearing. They were half a foot tall and deep in conversation. Their voices were high pitched, and I didn't understand the language.

They looked exactly like little humans. Their clothes were made of leaves of brown and green. One of them had a white flower in their hair.

Then I saw their wings. They were translucent and delicate and hung against their backs.

They were fairies! They were actual fairies!

I thought of Jonny and wished he was here. Part of me didn't care if it would mess with a plot. I had to bring Jonny to see them. He would be happy forever.

The fairies walked over to the mushrooms. They felled one of them with a tiny ax and bundled it into a net made of some woven plant.

They still hadn't seen me. I wanted to say hello. I wanted them to come up to me and talk to me in those little voices.

"Don't move," whispered the Librarian in my ear.

"Fairies!" I whispered back, turning to her.

"I know they are bloody fairies. Don't move a muscle."

"They are amazing."

"Amazing? There isn't anything amazing about these blighters."

"They seem harmless."

"Oh yes, they all look harmless until they tie you up with their wee ropes. I mean, I was just taking a nap on the beach..."

I looked back into the clearing. The two fairies were looking at us.

"I think they see us," said the Librarian slowly, still staring.

The two fairies jumped into the air, their wings extending. They hovered for a moment, then turned and flew into the jungle. "They are flying away," I said.

"That is not good," said the Librarian, "we need to leave. We need to leave right now."

"But why?"

"Open your book, young Keeper. They will be rousing the queen's armies now. Thank goodness we have that book."

Reluctantly I opened the book and began to read. I looked up before we fell into the pages just in time to see a swarm of tiny people flying our way.

"That was too bloody close!" said the Librarian once we had landed again.

"There were hundreds of them! How did they gather so fast?"

"There is not a fairy in all the multiverse that would have been able to resist the temptation of two travelers, alone in a jungle. Especially if one of them is a gorilla, apparently. I don't know why. There aren't fairies in Paris, are there?"

"I think there probably are," I said.

Once back in my bedroom, tiredness washed over me. I have heard that when you dream, you process all the new information you have taken in during the day. Judging by all the places I had been and everything I had seen, there would be plenty for me to process that night.

I lay back in my bed and started to doze off, still fully dressed.

That's when something caught my eye.

A blur of movement flew overhead. I sat up, my heart racing. I looked about the room, hoping, begging for it not to be what I thought it was.

Nothing.

I was just about to lay back down when another blur of movement caught my attention. This time it was unmistakable. There, walking tiptoe across the top of my laptop monitor, was a tiny person, dressed in clothes of leaves, with two translucent wings shimmering on its back.

CHAPTER 12

Slowly, I swung my legs over the side of the bed and got to my feet. It didn't seem like the fairy had noticed me yet.

How did it get through?

It must have been in my hair, or my bag, or something. The Librarian's warning about not messing up the stories was still fresh in my mind.

I crept forward, closer, and closer. Soon I was almost close enough to reach out and grab it. All I needed to do was capture the fairy and get it back to its own world before the Librarian noticed.

If she found out about the breach, then maybe she would just find another Keeper? Or Maybe The Library won't let me back in?

The fairy spun on its tiptoe and spotted me.

We locked eyes.

I smiled in what I hoped was a friendly, non-threatening kind of way. We were frozen for a moment.

I lunged forward.

Swift as anything, the fairy was in the air and buzzing overhead. That's when I noticed that my door was open ajar. I darted toward it, trying to close it before the fairy flew through, but it was almost too fast for my eyes to track. The fairy zipped out the door just moments before I slammed it shut.

I became aware that it was late at night, and I had just slammed the door. It was late at night, and a fairy had just escaped into my house.

What even is life right now.

As quietly as I could, I opened the door and peered out into the hallway. All was quiet, and there was no sign of the creature. I left my door open a little, just in case the fairy flew back in, and I could trap it.

I took a step forward and listened. Was that a rustle? Something dropping to the floor?

Was I hearing things?

Then there was a definite crash. It came from Jonny's room. I had to get it out of there before he woke up. If Jonny stirred and saw a real-life fairy in his room, there was no way I could keep him quiet.

I edged open his bedroom door and stepped in. It was dark, and only a slither of light crept in from the hallway. By the looks of things, Jonny was fast asleep.

Good, but where was the fairy?

Another crash. I turned around to see the fairy rummaging through a mug full of pens. It appeared to be looking for something.

"Stop that," I said.

The fairy poked its tongue out at me and flew directly at my face. I tried to grab it, but it was too fast. The fairy kicked me in the head and flew behind me. The kick didn't hurt, but it was really annoying.

I spun around and saw that the fairy was now on Jonny's pillow, investigating his face.

"Get away from there," I hissed.

It looked at me and then smiled the most wicked smile that ever I saw.

It was holding a pen.

It was swinging a pen.

I got to it moments before it would have jammed the pen into Jonny's ear.

He stirred in his sleep but did not wake. I looked up in time to see the fairy flying out into the hall. I hurried after it as quickly as I could, closing the bedroom door carefully behind me.

There was a blur of motion heading downstairs. I followed. The stairs creaked to an unreasonable degree. It was like they were trying to get me caught.

I got to the foot of the stairs and then stopped. The kitchen light was on, and there were the very definite sounds of Dad rummaging in the fridge.

There was no sign of the fairy.

I crept through the lounge and crouched down behind the couch. I listened as hard as I could, but the only thing I could hear was Dad's humming.

Where was the fairy?

The fridge door closed, and the kitchen light went out. Dad walked into the lounge, balancing a collection of fridge items and snack foods on a plate with one hand and holding two mugs of tea with the other.

It wouldn't take much for all that to fall.

I closed my eyes and prayed to whatever fairy god there was that my visitor would stay put for just one minute while Dad brought his treasure back to his den.

There was a flash of movement. The fairy was heading right for his legs. I almost shouted out to warn him, but that would only make things worse. All I could do was wait and watch for the collision to occur.

"Whoops," said Dad, swaying a little. I held my breath as I waited for a clatter of plates and mugs and humus.

It didn't come.

Slowly I edged my head out from behind the couch and saw that Dad was continuing his way up the stairs. The fairy must have missed, or maybe it was heading elsewhere.

I could see the fairy now. It was browsing Dad's collection of James Bond DVDs. He never watched them because we didn't have a DVD player of any kind, but considered such a collection to be essential.

Silent as I could, step after step, I crept towards the intruder. It didn't seem to know I was there.

Or so I thought.

The fairy yanked two DVDs from their cases and held them in each hand like weapons, dual-wielding. It growled a savage and slightly adorable growl.

"Just try it," I said.

CHAPTER 13

I squinted at the fairy and prepared to grab it.

The fairy dropped the DVDs and flew up until it was just beneath the ceiling and well out of my grasp. I looked about for something to reach it with. I didn't want to hurt the poor thing. It was probably terrified, but I couldn't help it get back home unless I caught it first.

It flew across the room to the top of our old bookcase, curled up, and appeared to go to sleep.

"Huh."

Well, at least it wasn't flying about the place and throwing things. I wasn't looking forward to tidying up the James Bond collection.

I grabbed a chair from the dining room and placed it down next to the bookcase. Once I had clambered up, I quickly swept the top of the bookcase, grabbing for the fairy.

I got it!

The fairy tried to pull away, but I had it by the leg. My mind was on the stairs now. I just had to get it back upstairs and to my book. Even if I just got it to The Library, then that had to be better than having it flying around my house.

That momentary distraction was all it needed. The

fairy bent down towards my hand and sunk its teeth deep into my thumb.

The pain was enormous.

Before I knew what I was doing, I had shaken the fairy off, and it was once again free. I darted after it as quick as I could.

Then I saw that there was still a window open in the kitchen.

The fairy took one last look at me, hovering at the window sill, and then flew away into the night.

***

Hank tormented me all the way to school. The Library was wonderful. Perhaps it was too wonderful. How could I have already jeopardized my chances of being a Keeper?

I pictured opening up Alice and just reading like it was any other old book. I pictured the puzzled Librarian explaining to the next Keeper how some of their predecessors just 'disappeared.'

I was almost afraid to try going back there. At least if I did not try, then I would not know whether or not I had lost that wonderful place forever.

School was a welcome distraction from my spiral of thoughts.

Even gym was welcome.

Gym class is where they teach you that physical exercise doesn't have to be fun. I mean, I get that some people enjoy sports, but I have absolutely no idea why.

I simply cannot fathom it.

If Mr. Wilson were to suggest hiking in the woods or running in the rain, then I'd look forward to his class. But for reasons that I don't understand, those activities are not a part of the regular curriculum.

"Everyone in alphabetical order, please," said Mr. Wilson.

Lilly ignored him and kept talking. "So anyway, I know that it's not normally your thing, but I was thinking it would totally be cool if we went on a double date with some boys."

"What? Why? Who?" I stammered.

"You would make a great reporter, Alex."

"Explain yourself, human."

"Well, I was going to see if you would like to go on a blind date, but I can't be bothered with that, so I'll just tell you. With Daniel and Carl."

"Which one would I be, um, dating?"

"Does it matter? Which one do you want?"

"Neither of them," I said flatly, though to be honest, I wasn't even sure that I didn't want to date. Dating is another thing I don't understand. It involves other humans, typically, and as such, was completely outside my sphere of experience.

"Good, then we are on the same page. It's not about them, really. I just think it's about time we get some practice in. You know, in case someone we do like comes along."

"That's a pretty long term thought, Lilly."

"I know, are you proud of me?"

"Well, seeing as this plan involves me socializing with strangers, I can't say that I'm all that proud."

"They are not strangers, they are Daniel and Carl."

I gave Lilly the 'everyone are strangers' look.

"Fine," said Lilly, "you can choose where we go."

"Lilly, I said alphabetical order. Last time I checked B and R were not next to each other in the alphabet!" said Mr. Wilson.

"Movies?" I ventured. I could already feel my stomach tying itself into knots and my mind trying to find an escape route.

"Does that even count?"

"Lilly!" shouted Mr. Wilson.

"Fine," she said and then turned to the teacher. "It is absolutely absurd of you to suggest that the alphabet needs to be in order," she proclaimed. "It's not as though words would change if the order of the alphabet changed," she then spun back to face me. "Oh, what if it does?!"

So now I had a date thing to worry about. I think that this is why people invented books. Life is full of awkwardness and obligation, but at least between two pages, I could escape. I could kind of tell in my heart that there was only a fifty-fifty chance that I would even go on this date with Lilly and the humans.

Lilly suggested we get a Sunday afternoon show so that at least we didn't use up a precious weekend evening. I knew what she was doing. She was doing her best to try and make sure I didn't freak out, as even now, I could see was probably going to happen.

***

I was sitting in history class when I saw it.

Staring out the window is a pretty standard activity for me in history class. This was not because I didn't enjoy history. As a matter of fact, it was one of my favorite classes. I just get easily distracted by the contents of my own mind.

The fairy flew right past the window, circled back, and then disappeared behind the oak tree in the courtyard.

"Shoot," I said.

"What was that, Alexandria?" asked Mr. Stewart.

"Sorry, may I be excused?"

Soon I was out of my class and fast-walking down the hallway. I knew better than to run. I couldn't afford to draw attention to myself. Maybe the fairy would come willingly? After all, it must be pretty lonely without any others of its kind around.

When I was outside, I headed for the oak tree and investigated its branches. The tree was in full sight of the classrooms, and I didn't want to look like a crazy person, but it was almost impossible to do anything in the courtyard without the possibility of being spotted.

There was no sign of my otherworldly visitor.

CHAPTER 14

I happened to glance up at my history classroom at the same time as Jake Sawyer happened to look out. He smiled stupidly and waved at me. I didn't actually know him, but he knew how to get people in trouble.

That's when I spotted it again. The fairy was flying into the administration building. I walked towards it as fast as I dared. Walk with purpose, and people will think you are meant to be there, right?

This was unknown territory. I had never had much reason to go into the administration building. There could be armed guards in there, for all I knew. Inside, the hallway was different from the school hallways. It was carpeted, which immediately changed the atmosphere. A phone was ringing in some unattended office.

There was no sign of the visitor.

I picked a door at random and walked in. I found myself in the teacher's staff room. It was empty. I breathed a sigh of relief. It was still not the sort of place I wanted to linger for long, though. I did a quick scan of the room.

Nothing unusual.

I was just about to leave when the sound of footsteps

and voices made me freeze. Someone was coming right this way. I quickly looked about for some legitimate reason why I might be in the staff room and saw the coffee machine.

Almost tripping over a chair, I stumbled towards it, grabbed a cup, and pressed a button.

Two adults whom I did not recognize walked in. They were deep in conversation, and, at first, did not realize I was there. I contemplated not moving, just in case they left without seeing me. But it wasn't to be.

"Oh, hello," said one woman. She looked like she might have been an accounts person.

"Hi," I said.

"I don't think you are supposed to be here," she said.

"I just needed to get a drink for Mr. Stewart," I said.

"And Mr. Stewart wants hot water does he?"

I looked down at the polystyrene cup I was holding and at the clear hot liquid it contained. I had somehow pressed the only button which wouldn't give me coffee.

"Yeah," I said, "I better go."

"I wish I had a kid to fetch me drinks," said the other lady as I left.

Great, so now I had lost the fairy again and had a cup of boiling water to carry around. I was just about ready to go back to class at this point. I would just have to tell the Librarian that a fairy escaped into my world. She would understand. She hated fairies, right?

The cup of hot water was stressing me out. As soon as I was outside, I placed the cup on the first flat surface I could find.

Then I saw the fairy. It flew out the school gates and

across the street.

This was exhausting. I did not have an adrenal system suitable for this sort of work. What if I did just leave it? What's the worst that could happen?

I imagined an eight-foot gorilla kicking me out of the magic library at the center of all creation.

This time I ran.

If I was going to catch the fairy, then I needed to be serious about it. It's not as though school was that important anyway. I already had my career lined up at The Library. And, even if it didn't pay much, at least I would have a place to sleep.

I followed the blur of movement down the road and then down a side street. Where was it going?

It flew uphill now. The fairy had the significant advantage of flight. There was another oak tree ahead. Maybe it liked oak trees?

Just as it got close, it turned around and saw that it was being followed. It didn't seem at all concerned. In fact, it looked like it was laughing at me.

Its expression turned to puzzlement as my face dropped in horror.

A cat leaped from its vantage position in the tall grass and clawed the fairy to the ground.

"Bad kitty!" I said, and ran forward.

Big mistake.

The cat was off like a rocket, the fairy hanging limply in its mouth.

This was worse, definitely much worse. The cat sprinted down a path. About halfway down, it leaped onto a fence and then down into someone's backyard.

I tried to see over, but the fence was too high, and I was frankly terrible at jumping. I would have to go around. I cringed at the thought of being caught creeping around someone's backyard, but the thought of being caught wasn't nearly as bad as the thought of poor fairy dying.

It was kind of my fault too.

If I hadn't distracted it from its oak-related mission, then it wouldn't have let its guard down.

The front of the house was on the next road over. I made careful observations of its steep black roofing and white-bordered windows and hurried around to find the house that matched. It didn't take me long.

I hesitated on the side of the road. There was a car in the driveway. This definitely meant someone was home.

There was nothing else for it. I crept as inconspicuously as I could along the fence line and into the backyard. It was quite a well-off street, and this family had a swimming pool. A vision of the fairy drowning at the bottom of the pool flashed before my mind's eye. I made a quick visual sweep of the watery depths.

Nothing there.

Then the cat let out the most bizarre and agonized meow I had ever heard. It was sitting expectantly at the back door with the fairy unmoving at its feet.

It meowed again.

There was noise within the house. The cat had summoned its master. There wasn't much time. I ran for the cat as fast as I could. It looked up at me, startled for a moment, and then bolted, leaving its trophy behind. I picked up the fairy and held it. It was pretty bloodied, but still breathing.

There was another sound from inside the house, this time right behind the door. I ran for the side of the house, out of sight. If I had been a moment slower then I would have been caught.

"Nothing. The damn cat seems to have brought us another present. It's gone through," said a man's voice.

When I was out on the street, I looked at the fairy more closely. I would have to take it to The Library now and get it back to its people. I was no nurse, and I was fairly sure that this would be beyond the expertise of most vets.

The problem was, my bag with my book was back in history class, and I was not. Mr. Stewart would definitely be wondering where I was now. A pang of anxiety rocketed through me as I wondered if history class was still actually going. I looked at my watch. There was still time left to get back. I just needed to find some way of getting the injured fairy inside unnoticed. Easy, right?

Moments later, I was walking in through the school gate, my sweater wrapped around the fairy, the wind blowing in my face, and goosebumps creeping up my arms.

CHAPTER 15

We missed you," said Mr. Stewart.

"Me too," I said, fumbling in my awkwardness. The class tittered at this apparent display of anti-authoritarianism.

"Alright, sit down."

I sat down at my desk, carefully holding the precious bundle on my lap. Now what was I supposed to do?

A quiet groan came from within my sweater's folds. I froze, looking about to see if anyone else had heard it. The poor thing was waking up. I had to get to The Library as soon as possible. As quietly as I could, I opened my bag. I would need to take some things out if I was to conceal the fairy properly.

That's when I noticed that my book was gone. My copy of Alice had disappeared.

My mind started to race. I looked suspiciously at the students that sat nearest my desk. None of them seemed to be the swiping type.

Did I even bring it to school?

I couldn't remember, but it was now more urgent than ever that I find it. Time seemed to stand still as I waited for class to be over. This wasn't my last class for the day, but I had no other choice. My book was probably just still at home. I needed to get there, and I needed to get there soon, or this creature would die bundled in my favorite sweater.

The bell rang.

I got up as quickly as I could and slung my bag awkwardly over my shoulder.

"Alexandria," said Mr. Stewart, just as I was walking through the door. I should have kept going. I turned around instinctively.

"Is everything OK?" he asked.

"Yeah, I'm fine."

"No, your not," he said urgently and coming forward, "you're bleeding."

I looked down at my hands. Fairy blood was smeared where I had picked it up. I was so worried about getting the fairy back that I had forgotten to wipe the blood off.

"Oh, shoot," I said, trying to appear shocked. "I was afraid this would happen. I gotta go."

"By all means, yes, go," he said, stumbling over his words, "I hope it all turns out," he added.

It wasn't a long walk home, but it was longer than I would have liked. In my frazzled imagination, every car that passed was potentially one of my parents or some friend of the family ready to pull over and wonder at me being out of school. I could feel my whole body tense up as the cars approached and relax when they passed.

At last, I was home. I opened the door and ran upstairs. Mom wouldn't be home until Jonny had finished school. I had ample time to get into The Library, return the fairy, and be back in time to clean up.

The stairs thudded as I ran to my room.

I lay the fairy out on the bed and went to grab my book from my side table. It wasn't there. I looked at the bookshelf, and it wasn't there either. It wasn't by my desk, it wasn't on the floor. I turned the room upside down trying to find my book, but it simply wasn't anywhere.

Had I brought it to school after all? I rechecked my bag. Nothing there.

Time was running out for my visitor.

I had no choice but to try and help it myself. I ran to the bathroom cupboard and grabbed everything that looked like it might be useful. I soaked a flannel in warm water and ran back to my bedroom. I turned on the light and examined my patient.

I really had no idea what I was looking at. Delicately, I wiped away the dried blood. The fairy was tossing and turning in its unconscious state. There appeared to be a small puncture wound in its abdomen and a series of wounds on one of its legs. The abdominal puncture scared me. I didn't know much about human anatomy, but if fairies were anything like people, then there were lots of important bits in that area. All I could do was clean up the wound and bind it best I could.

"Sorry," I said as I wiped the injuries down with an antiseptic wipe. The fairy flinched. I wrapped a bandage around its midsection and used pieces of plaster tape on the cuts on its leg. By the time I was done, the fairy looked like it was made up more of household medical supplies than organic matter.

I cleared away the rest of the bandages and the first aid kit, trying to make it look like it had never been touched in the first place. The last thing I needed was for Mom to be asking questions about who had been into her supplies. Then I washed up my hands and put my sweater in the washing machine. With any luck, it would be done before Mom got home.

Now that the fairy was out of immediate danger, I sat down to fret. Where could the book possibly be? How could I have lost it after so short a time as a Keeper? Not much of a Keeper, I guess.

A Loser?

I searched my room again. It looked like a small tornado had started somewhere near my desk and had terrorized my bed and the rest of the room before dying away.

Then it struck me: what if Mom had it?

Relief washed over me. Mom probably had it!

But what if Mom read it?

There was no point to the speculating, and yet my mind did it anyway. I pictured Mom coming home and telling me that she had met this gorilla and that they had really hit it off. Then I pictured my Mom thumping the gorilla with her purse and telling it to keep its own library.

It seemed like an eternity waiting.

I anxiously watched the clock, checking on the fairy every few minutes. Time inevitably ticked, and Mom inevitably came home.

"Hi, Mom," I said as I ran down the stairs. She hadn't even gotten in the door.

"You're home early," she said, "what are you washing?"

I had forgotten to take my sweater out of the machine. Too late now. "Oh, my sweater. I got mud on it."

"Mud? How did you manage that?"

"An unfortunate... mud-related-incident..." I said, "anyway. My book, have you seen my book?"

"Hi Alex!" said Jonny, skipping into the house.

"Shoes, Jonny!" said Mom, "you seem eager." She was being evasive.

I grew tense.

"Mom, where is my book?"

"I didn't think you would miss it. I mean, you were at school, so I just thought I'd-"

"What did you do?" my heart was racing now.

"Don't get shirty with me. I just took it in to get appraised. First editions are worth a lot of money, Alex."

"I don't want money, Mom. I want my book."

"You might not always feel like that. Anyway, it wasn't supposed to take this long. Mr. O'Conner at Albany Antiques was supposed to give me a call this afternoon, but he hasn't gotten back to me."

"We have to go down there."

"What are you so worried about? He probably just got a little busy. I'm sure I'll be able to get it back to you tomorrow morning. And really, Alex. I did this for you. Surely you wanted to know if it was valuable?"

"I already knew that it was valuable. Can we just go now, please? I need it for my oral presentation," I lied.

"Oh - well, I'm sorry, Alex, but we can't. Albany Antiques closes early. You will just have to be patient."

"Patient?!"

CHAPTER 16

Exasperated, I stormed upstairs. I could feel tears welling up in my eyes. I just wanted to do the right thing, but everything was a mess. Why did Mom have to interfere with everything like this?

I knew Mr. O'Connor from going into the store with Mom. He was in his nineties. He was probably already perusing the mystery section of The Library. If he could find it.

What if he died from the shock of being teleported into a different dimension? I pictured the Librarian walking up to him, dead on the tiles, prodding him with a massive leathery finger.

I couldn't wait.

There was too much at stake. Albany wasn't close by, but at least it was within walking distance. I didn't know exactly what I would do when I got there, but I had to try and get my book back.

I carefully placed the fairy in my sock drawer. It was burning up. I felt so sad to see its pain. That sadness drove me on.

I found an old jacket with a hood, grabbed my phone, and started out the door. It would be almost dark by the time I got there. I plugged myself into headphones and walked as quickly as I could.

I was warm by the time I got to Albany Antiques. It was a shabby one-story shop. It always puzzled me as a child why a place that contained such beautiful objects looked so tatty from the outside.

The front door had a distinct aura of solidness about it. I tried the handle.

It didn't budge.

I walked around the building, looking for an open window. I felt nervous about being in a place where I shouldn't be.

Hank was definitely wide awake.

Out the back of the shop, there was a gravel yard and a few old cars. It didn't look like people came back here very often.

The weeds were making a valiant effort to reclaim this land.

It seemed to be the sort of place where you might find broken glass, so I walked as carefully as I could. There were no open windows out the back of the building, either.

I was about to try the other side of the building when I saw that there was a garage door. It was open a crack at its base.

I tucked my hands inside my jacket sleeves to avoid cutting myself on something rusty and tried to pull the door upward. It creaked and moaned and moved up a few inches. The sound was loud in the quiet evening. I looked about nervously and then pulled again.

Soon it was high enough for me to crawl under. I lowered myself to the ground and switched on the light on my phone to see what was on the other side.

My torch illuminated a sea of dust swirling around in the darkness. It looked like your typical barely-used garage and smelled distinctly of engine oil.

I found a spot where the ground seemed the cleanest and pulled my way through. Once on the other side, I began to really appreciate just how messy a garage could get.

An old car took up most of the space. It looked like it was in only slightly better condition than those left outside. There was hardly enough room for me to inch passed it to get to the door. Once passed, I grabbed at the brass door handle.

It opened.

I breathed a sigh of relief and stepped into the shop. It was quite dark now, and only a small amount of light penetrated through the windows. They looked like they had never been cleaned. I had been in this store many times during the day, but never alone, and never at night. A stillness hung over everything.

I cast the light of my phone over the room. Brass objects polished within an inch of existence gleamed back at me.

This place was like a treasure cave.

Ancient ships lanterns hung from the rafters, sailing on the silent seas. Gramophones were playing hushed melodies to each other. There were ornate weighing devices, kept by some loving hands from before the switch to electricity.

The shop was a shrine to the god of ornate craftsmanship.

There was also something about this place that reminded me of a graveyard. Each of these objects was like a headstone for its original owner, long passed away.

I loved it here.

If it weren't for the urgency of my expedition, I would certainly have lingered. I wasn't really into the whole breaking and entering thing, but I made a mental note to ask Mr. O'Connor if I could come here to read sometime after he had closed down for the night.

If Mr. O'Connor was still alive.

I crept to the front desk and started searching all the places one might leave a book. The place was a mess. It could have been anywhere.

The piercing light of headlights swept across the shop, accompanied by the unmistakable sound of a car parking.

I froze.

A car door was opened and then closed again. There was the rattle of keys. I ducked down behind the front desk and turned off my phone's light.

The door lock clicked open.

There was nothing I could do. I was crouched in the most obvious location, and there was no way I could get out. All I could do was stay there, frozen, hoping that whoever it was would go away.

The shop light switched on, flooding everything with a soft yellow light. I listened carefully, trying to hear something, anything which would betray this person's movements.

The light switched off. The door was closed again. The

car outside started, and its headlights blinked on. It drove away.

I realized that I had been holding my breath.

Mr. O'Connor needed a better security guy.

I waited a few more moments, just in case they came back.

When it was clear that I was alone, I switched my phone light back on and continued my search. I was frantic. I checked under every piece of paper, opened every drawer, and scanned every shelf. Finally, I sat back in the chair, exasperated, defeated.

That's when I saw it. There, off to one side, was another door. Another freaking door. How did I miss that?

Feelings of relief washed over me. I got to my feet and darted for the door. I turned the handle expecting it to come open, but it wouldn't budge.

"Shoot."

There was a glass window in the door. I shone my light through. It looked to be some kind of workroom. It seemed to be the place where the restorations were done.

There, on the desk, was a book.

CHAPTER 17

I stayed in the antiques store for another hour, ignoring the increasingly dramatic texts from my mother, but there was no way into that room. Dejected, I started the long walk back home.

All I could think about was that little creature. I had this image of finding it dead in my sock drawer in the morning. It was just so sad, but I couldn't think about anything else. I had failed it. The Librarian was wrong. I was not fit to be The Library's Keeper.

When I got home, Mom was pointedly waiting for me. "Where have you been?" she demanded.

"Out," I said, trying to dodge her and get upstairs.

"Don't just 'out' me, missy. That's not good enough. This is a school night. Jonny has been asking where you are."

I looked over at Jonny. He was eating an apple and watching TV, oblivious.

"Sorry, I just had to go. Lilly has a copy of Alice."

"Well, you need to tell me, not just shoot off like that. I don't like this sort of behavior, Alexandria. I don't want to see it becoming a habit."

"Look, I'm sorry. Can I go?"

"Just text me next time."

Soon I was at the top of the stairs and then in my bedroom. I turned on the light to see that my window was open, and the fairy was standing on the ledge. It looked at me, clearly still in pain.

But it was alive. I breathed a sigh of relief.

"Go," I said, "just watch out for cats, OK? Come back when you want to go home."

The fairy nodded and then flew into the night, a loose bandage trailing behind.

***

I hardly slept that night.

My brain whirred as I thought over all the things I could say to the Librarian to try and convince her that something like this wouldn't happen again.

When I awoke, my head was thudding. I got ready for school as normal, but as soon as I was out of the house, I started walking towards Albany and the antiques store. So I would be late for school? This was far more important.

The roads were clogged up with commuters heading into the city. I felt self-conscious and exposed walking in the opposite direction to school. All I could do was focus on walking forward.

It was 10 am when I arrived at Albany Antiques. If anything, it looked even more run-down in the morning light.

To my dismay, it was still not open. I looked about for something indicating the opening hours. Why hadn't I checked that last night?

After a few moments of searching, I found a sticker on the window. It had peeled in the heat and was almost impossible to read. I couldn't see what the opening hours on Friday were supposed to be, but if they were the same as the rest of the week, then they were definitely late opening up.

What if they never opened?

I leaned against the wall and waited. After a while, my phone buzzed.

Where were you?

It was Lilly. I had forgotten to tell her not to wait for me out the front of the school. Knowing Lilly, she probably missed the first class waiting there.

Sorry, I'll tell you about it later. Sorry.

There was no reply. I felt pretty guilty. Lilly and I had a pretty robust friendship, and she was used to me flaking out, but it still sucks to let people down.

At last, a car pulled up and parked outside the shop. I felt super awkward standing there and waiting. I imagined what was going on in the driver's head and cringed. But I had no choice. I needed to get in there and get out as soon as possible.

A woman stepped out of the car. "Good morning!" she said with an unnatural degree of cheerfulness.

"Morning," I said.

She unlocked the door to the shop, stepped inside, and turned on the lights. I hesitated and then stepped in after her.

She sat behind the desk, and I became painfully aware of all the rummaging I had done there the night before and hoped that I had put everything back right. Would she suspect me if anything was out of place?

"Just give me a second," she said. She unlocked the workshop door, disappeared for a moment, and then came back and sat back down. "Now, what can I do for you?"

"Um, my mom brought a book here yesterday to be appraised. I need to get it back."

"What was the name of the book?" she asked.

"Alice's Adventures in Wonderland."

"Yes, well, our appraiser isn't in yet. He usually unlocks. He must be running late."

"That's OK, I just need the book back."

"What did you say your name was?"

"Alex Reed. My mom, Jane Reed, brought it in yesterday but didn't hear back. I need it today for school."

"That shouldn't be a problem. Do you have the receipt?"

My heart skipped a beat. "Receipt? No, I-"

"I'm terribly sorry. I can't hand over anything without evidence that it is yours. You understand. We can't have just anyone walking in off the street and claiming valuable antiques, now can we?"

"But I have to have it!" I blurted.

"I'm sorry. I suppose I could call your mother?"

"No, I mean- "

"No?"

"OK, sure. Give her a call."

The woman gave me a suspicious look and then started thumbing through some sort of vintage phone number filing system. "Jane, isn't it," she said, more to herself.

"Yes."

I could hear the phone ringing from where I was standing. Mom would probably want to 'have a talk' when I got home.

"Mrs. Reed? Yes, hi, this is Caroline from Albany Antiques - No, I'm afraid Mr. O'Connor isn't in yet. This is concerning your daughter... Yes, your daughter, Alex, isn't it?" she made an eyebrow gesture at me, and I nodded. "Well, she is here at the store... Yes, she is... I was wondering about that. We don't get many school students here during the day. Or at all, come to that... Yes, well, she has come to pick up the book you left with us yesterday. I was just telling her that Mr. O'Connor has not finished his report, and... Are you sure?... OK, that's fine... OK, until next time. Bye."

I waited expectantly as Caroline hung up the call.

"I'll just get it from out back."

Relief washed over me. A few moments later, the woman came back and handed me the book. It was amazing to have it in my hands again.

"A beautiful book," she said, with longing, "where did you get it?"

"Just a book shop."

"What a find. Well, I hope you appreciate it. I know people who would kill for a book like that."

CHAPTER 18

I hurried back to school as fast as I could, trying not to think about the kinds of people who would kill to have access to The Library.

I resisted the temptation to dive into The Library and start searching for Mr. O'Connor. I was late enough as it was, and the last thing I needed right now was more trouble at school.

As I walked through the front gate, I glanced about to see if anyone would see me enter. I was still early enough to make it to one morning class, at least, and there was always a chance that nobody would notice that the quiet girl who sat at the back of the class was missing.

Just when it seemed like I had gotten away without trouble, I caught the eye of a teacher walking by.

It was Mr. Wilson.

He didn't smile or nod or anything, but I knew he had seen me. I suspected that I was fast becoming his least favorite student, but I couldn't worry about that now. I just had to get to class.

All through math class, my mind was on The Library. It was a massive place, and Mr. O'Connor could be anywhere. I tried to imagine where a ninety-year-old antiques dealer would wander but came up with no obvious answers. There was a strong possibility that I would have to come clean and let the Librarian know that I messed up.

When lunchtime came, I didn't stick around. I maybe should have apologized to Lilly again, but The Library was just more important right now.

I fast-walked across the empty sports field. The sanctuary was quiet and welcoming.

Books had many times transported me to another world here, but usually not so literally. I found a large tree to put my bag behind, sat down, and opened to the first chapter.

As soon as I landed in The Library, I began my search. The Librarian didn't seem to be around. Good. Maybe I could get this done quietly. My first idea was to go to the maps area. There were several old cabinets there which he would definitely be interested in. But when I got there, it was just as empty as ever. An image flashed in my mind's eye of Mr. O'Connor, stumbling and falling into The Library's canyon.

No, he was old, not blind.

I ran down the stairs and to the observatory. Empty as well.

Was I going to have to search every shelf? I tried to keep on moving. I only had to be right once, and then I would be able to send him back to my world. I searched and searched, but it was no use. The Library was just too big, and I simply did not have enough time to search everywhere. Lunchtime would be finishing soon. Where was he?

The sound of laughter made me stop.

I listened hard to see where it was coming from. There was the sound of two people talking. I followed the noise. It led me down a flight of stairs and to the room where the Librarian had taken me after she first found me.

Cautiously, I crept in.

There, sitting opposite each other, was the Librarian and Mr. O'Connor. The Librarian's armchair was significantly larger than the other. They appeared to be drinking tea and having a laugh. I walked in, and their conversation hushed.

"Little Miss Reed!" said Mr. O'Connor. He stood up, walked toward me, and took my hand. "I should have known you would end up in a place like this. I still remember you as a little girl. You always had a book tucked under one arm. Oh, how sweetly you would sit in one of my old chairs while your mother looked about. You never did heed the do-not-sit signs. I would suggest you couldn't read them, but I think you probably read more than I did. I never had the heart to tell you to get off. And now here you are, a library of your own!"

"I was just keeping our guest company until you arrived," said the Librarian, "we actually have quite a lot in common."

I didn't know what to say or do. Mr. O'Connor was acting like a magical library inside a book was the most normal thing in the world, and the Librarian was acting as if him being there was no problem at all.

"Hi," I said.

"You seem embarrassed," said Mr. O'Connor, "come, sit! Have a cup of tea. We are old friends, you and I. A secret library, eh? Can't be many of these around."

"Um..."

"I did know one family who had a magical wardrobe, actually. Never went in myself, but I heard a lot about it. I have to say, a magical library is a far better idea. I mean, what use is a whole dimension full with coats?" he turned to the Librarian, "that place was run by a lion, apparently. Had the awful habit of falling asleep for weeks at a time. There was this one time when they thought he was dead, and-"

"I'm sorry, Mr. O'Connor. But I have to take you back. I'm at school, and lunch is almost over."

"Go back?" he looked from me to the Librarian and back to me again.

I looked to the Librarian. She smiled.

"Oh, just let him stay another day. I don't get many people to talk to here, you know. And he is such a nice young man."

"That's very kind of you to say," said Mr. O'Connor, taken aback.

"It's nothing, really," said the Librarian.

Did she just blush?

"Right," I said. There was clearly something else going on here that I didn't quite understand. "I'll be going then."

"Be sure to stop by later!" said Mr. O'Connor.

Soon I was back in the sanctuary. The last couple of days had been a real roller coaster, and contrary to all my predictions, everything seemed to be turning out OK. I mean, the fairy was still at large, but at least it was alive.

I slumped against a tree and closed my eyes.

Immediately, I opened them again. There were voices.

I was not alone.

It sounded like Mr. Wilson and Mr. Daniels were on lunchtime duty again. From my position behind the old oak tree, I could smell the smoke from their cigarettes wafting on the wind. It seemed like they had their own reasons for wanting to escape the jungle that was the schoolyard.

For a moment, I considered retreating back into my book, but it was so close to the end of lunchtime. I had no choice.

I had to sneak by.

I hung low to the ground, trying to stay out of sight. Whatever it was that the teachers were talking about seemed to have them quite animated. It was possible I was going to make it! I quickened my pace.

I must have made a sound because they both looked up at once.

"Alex Reed," said Mr. Wilson, his voice level.

CHAPTER 19

Mr. Wilson pressed his cigarette butt into the earth with his foot. Mr. Daniels hurriedly tried to do the same. "What did we tell you about coming here out of bounds? We have very strict drug policies here, Miss Reed."

"I was reading."

"A bit sly of you to stay quiet for all this time," Mr. Daniels stammered, "you didn't hear anything you shouldn't have, did you?"

"I don't know," I said, wondering what I shouldn't have heard.

"Regardless, you have earned yourself detention," said Mr. Wilson, "tomorrow morning. Be there or be in severe trouble."

"But-," I said. I know I go red when I am embarrassed, but right then, I felt like I was going a deep shade of purple.

"Just get to class," said Mr. Daniels.

With my book clutched to my chest, I hurried away, turmoil in my heart.

***

The clock seemed to tick at half speed during my last class. Time simply refused to pass. I just wanted to get back to The Library.

I had to escape from this stupid place.

When the bell rang, I hurried out of the school grounds. I wanted to forget about the detention and get lost someplace wonderful. Once home, I sat cross-legged on my bed and opened my book.

I passed the Librarian walking down a central aisle. She carried a huge stack of books balanced in her sturdy arms. They looked heavy. I suppose being a gorilla has its perks.

"Hello there. Where is Mr. O'Connor?"

"In the reading room. He is going to stay for a while to get some reading in. These are for him."

"Oh," I said, "is there anything I need to do today?"

"Nothing urgent. Familiarize yourself with the place, and see if you can feel the call of the books. Remember what I told you?"

"Yes, I remember. I'll do my best."

As much as I wanted to settle down and actually enjoy The Library for what it was, I couldn't help but explore this strange new land, my strange new land.

I soon realized that The Library was not uniform in its style. In the areas that I explored so far, everything was grand and traditional, everything in its place. Today I found places where the light subsided, and the rows of books fell away. The walls turned to large cement bricks, lit by torches.

I followed down one of these corridors for a short way. There was a distant drip-drip of water. The further I went, the darker it got. Hank started drumming on my heart. I lost my nerve and turned back.

I came to a blazing fireplace. A couple of couches were set around it. It reminded me of a ski lodge, a warm island in a world of snow. The fire crackled invitingly. A mug of what looked like hot cocoa was steaming on a coffee table. I was about to sit down when I heard a crash.

What on earth could that be?

There was another crash. I walked toward the sound, quickening my pace. When I was close, I started to hear the distinct sound of muttering. I thought I was alone?

Another crash.

There were books strewn everywhere. Many had fallen open and had their pages bent. Some deep instinctual part of me revolted.

The muttering was coming from somewhere up a ladder. I looked up to see a woman frantically grabbing every book within reach, looking at its cover, and then tossing it over her shoulder. Some more confident version of myself might have said 'that's no way to judge a book.'

I slowly backed away.

With speed that unnerved me, the woman leaped from the top of the ladder and landed hard on the tiled ground, still holding one of the books.

The sound of several bones clicking into or out of place echoed as she stood up. In honesty, it was more like she was unfolding. She eyed me with small suspicious eyes. I had never met a woman who looked so old in all my life. She was frankly terrifying.

"And who might you be?" the woman demanded,

"have you got it?"

She seemed a little unhinged. "Got what?" I croaked.

"Don't play coy with me. Have you got my book?"

"Which book is that?" I was tense, and my voice was quivering. Did she mean Alice? My hand moved to cover my bag.

"The bloody book with my bloody face on the front!" she screeched, "where is it?"

"I don't know. I am new here."

The old woman leaned in close so that her eyes were only inches from my own. It seemed like she was trying to read my thoughts through my pupils.

"Well, if you see it, you will let me know, won't you?" she pushed a book into my chest. Instinctively I grabbed it. She turned and made her way muttering up the ladder with considerably less drama than when she had come down.

I looked at the book I was now holding. Etched into the cover was the unmistakable face of the dreadful old woman. She had just handed it to me. I opened my mouth to say something but then realized that I would much rather run away.

So I did.

CHAPTER 20

I think you ran into our visitor," said the Librarian when I found her.

"Yes. I thought I was the only one here."

"Ordinarily, that would be true, but this - well, she's a special case."

"Who is she?"

"She is just an old woman with a lifetime of regrets. We get them now and then. Not too frequently, mind you. They wander out of their stories when they are truly lost. Is she looking for her book?"

"She handed it to me." I held up the book for the Librarian to see.

She laughed. "That would be about right!"

"Why would she hand me the book if she is looking for it?"

"Remember, Alex, the books aren't just books. They are lives. Even your story is on one of these shelves somewhere, but you will never find it."

"How come?"

"We can never read our own stories. That's what our visitor is trying to do. She has most likely made some great errors in her life and is looking for a way to go back and change things. But that can never be. We can sometimes sense when our story is close at hand, but even if we look right at it, we will not recognize it as our own."

"So, she handed it to me."

"She handed it to you."

I took the book to the green couch that I found on my first day at The Library, next to the hanging window. The weather had cleared up somewhat, but the clouds still threatened rain. I had some regret as I remembered the hot cocoa and the fireplace, but I wasn't in the mood to go searching it out. There was no guarantee that I would ever find it again.

Just as I was getting comfortable, I heard a sound on the glass of the window. I looked out and saw a cat pawing gently at the pane. It was large and black and looked like it wanted to escape the coming weather.

"Hey kitty," I said, opening the window. The cat climbed down and onto the couch. I closed the window, and it swayed slightly on its chains.

Thankfully, the cat said nothing in reply. It just curled up next to me and fell asleep. It looked exactly like my grandma's cat. I stroked it gently.

I looked at the old woman's book and dusted off its cover. I wondered what sort of life she had led and how she had gotten into The Library. I felt the urge to have a look inside.

Was this the call of the book?

I closed my eyes and tried to focus on my feelings.

Nothing.

The Librarian had not been clear on what this feeling

was supposed to be. I certainly wanted to read the book. Surely that was good enough?

I opened it up and began to read. I braced myself, ready to fall into the pages, but nothing happened. It was just like any other book. Shrugging, I kept reading.

The story described a little girl called Elaine, who was all alone. She tried to make friends with the other children of the village, but they were mean to her. They called her freak and strange and threw rocks at her. From time to time, Elaine would become angry, and when she was angry, things would happen, which she could not explain.

One day, a boy named Sefton Carlwater threw mud at her and got it all over her new white dress. Elaine was so upset because she knew her mother would be sad to see the dress ruined, not angry, just sad.

And this was somehow worse.

She didn't mean for anything bad to happen, but when Sefton's hair caught fire, Elaine laughed as Sefton screamed. He eventually put the fire out in a little brown puddle. Elaine rejoiced to hear that Sefton's mother was sad as well.

After that, the people of the village called a meeting, and at that meeting, they decided to cast Elaine out of the village for good. Elaine was sad, and her mother was sad, and together, they cried.

Fortunately, Elaine had a sister called Tabatha, and she agreed to go with Elaine, for though Elaine did on occasions do some rather nasty things to her sister, Tabatha always forgave her because she loved her sister dearly, no matter how strange she got.

There did not appear to be any more written in the

book after that, though there were many more blank pages.

"What a peculiar story," I said to the cat. Its purrs had reached peak helicopter by this point.

CHAPTER 21

I closed Elaine's book and set it on a side table. I sat for a while, thinking about the story. Part of me wanted to find the old lady again and give her a hug.

My eyes fell on the landscape that stretched away out the window. I began to wonder what The Library looked like from outside. It was raining now, but I didn't mind it. I lifted the window up and poked my head outside.

I craned my neck, looking left and right. It seemed to me that The Library was in a castle, grand and old. The stones looked like they were crumbling in parts, and vines were growing up the brickwork. The air was clear and refreshing, and the smell of the rain on the old bricks filled my nostrils. It was like that smell that roads get in the summer after a shower.

"Are you alright there?" asked the Librarian from behind me.

Startled, I pulled my head back inside, banging it on the way in.

"Oh, yes," I said, rubbing the place that I had banged. There would be a lump for sure. "Um, I just wanted to ask about this book. I only read a chapter, and there doesn't seem to be any more."

"Ah, yes, that does happen sometimes. The book has a will of its own. It will only show you what it wants to show you. Self-preservation, I think. How did you find it?"

"I'm not sure. A little creepy, I think."

"I am not surprised."

"I better head back. Mom will wonder where I am. Can I check the book out?"

"You can check it out any time you want, but you may never leave," said the Librarian, grinning. She tapped her nose for good measure.

"Hotel California?"

"Yes, indeedy! I've been researching your culture. Very strange hotels you must have. But in all seriousness, no. You can't take them from The Library. They are reference only, you might say."

***

I very seriously considered not going to detention. I mean, what would happen if I just went to The Library every time people wanted me to do something that I didn't want to do? The Library offered a level of escape that I never thought possible.

It was changing my life forever.

On the morning of the detention, I decided I would go, but not without my book. I was determined to get out of the house before anyone was up, so I wouldn't get the third degree about the detention. It was stupid, I mean, who gives people detention for reading?

I couldn't tell my parents.

I imagined what it would be like telling Mom. I could vividly see her expression, her mingled concern and pity, that look that people give you when they know that you are defective.

I knew that it wasn't a great idea to bring Alice. The temptation to disappear during detention was probably going to be too great, but I stuffed it into my bag anyway. I didn't like the idea of Mom or Jonny randomly coming across it and finding out about the secret world within its pages.

I got to school early. When Mr. Wilson finally turned up, he just opened the door to one of the classrooms and then left me there without saying anything.

At first, I thought that I was just supposed to sit there for two hours in silence and boredom. People were always thinking up useful ways to use up your time like that.

After about ten minutes, Darcy walked in, Mr. Wilson behind him.

"I can't be here!" Darcy protested.

"You are lucky I didn't call the cops," said Mr. Wilson. This definitely seemed like a conversation they had had before.

"Come on, I need to go. There are things I need to do. People are depending on me."

"You had a weapon at school."

"It was after hours!"

"And you still haven't given me an adequate explanation as to why, Darcy. Until I get one, you will sit in this room with Miss Reed."

Darcy turned and saw me. He looked embarrassed, and I felt embarrassed for him being embarrassed.

"I have a task for the two of you," said Mr. Wilson. He placed a book on each of our desks. They were textbooks on Irish History. "You will find a collection of essay questions near the front of the book. Answer one of them."

"This is a waste of time."

"Yes, Darcy. It is a waste of time. I had to get up early on a Saturday morning for you, and you aren't even grateful." Mr. Wilson sighed. "Just do the essay."

Darcy kicked his desk in apparent frustration. I wondered what the desk had done to him to deserve this treatment.

"I'll be back soon," said Mr. Wilson. "Don't go anywhere."

Once Mr. Wilson had left, Darcy immediately got up and left the room too.

I was alone with the silent papers and distant morning birdsong. I opened the textbook and started reading. As far as detentions go, this didn't seem so bad. Mr. Wilson was a gym teacher, after all. He could have made us watch sports, or something.

It wasn't long before Mr. Wilson came back. He saw that Darcy was gone and immediately stormed off, swearing.

I wasn't sure about this Darcy guy. The Librarian seemed to think that he was in danger. He seemed alright. I mean, it was definitely interesting that he had a sword at school, but he seemed really serious and was mean to desks.

I felt the urge to take out my book, even just to place it

on my desk. At this point, I figured that Mr. Wilson would be tied up with finding Darcy. I opened to chapter one and began to read.

I couldn't stay in The Library long, but it was better than detention. My mind was on Elaine's book. I found myself worrying about the two little girls lost in the wilderness. I wanted to find them and help them.

When I got to my nook, I found that the cat was sitting there, waiting for me. It greeted me, and I petted its head. The book was right where I had left it.

The weather through the window was bright and sunny. I opened the book and began to read.

My peripheral went dark, and my heart stopped beating. The air drained from my lungs, and the page rushed towards me.

I was being pulled in.

I tried to withdraw my gaze, but it was too late. I was falling.

I landed on hard concrete. Darkness wrapped around me. I collapsed onto the ground, unable to see. The floor beneath me was cold and dusty. There was the distinct aroma of something dead somewhere nearby. I covered my mouth.

"Psst," said a voice.

I looked about but couldn't see anything. My eyes were adjusting, but still, everything was shadow.

"Over here," said the voice. Now, through the dim light, I could see her. It was a girl. She seemed to be a couple of years older than me. She was staring at me, eyes wide, both hands clinging to the bars of her prison cell. "Quickly!"

"What is it?" I said, uncertain. My heart was pounding fast, and I did not want to be here. Hank was going berserk.

"The guard is asleep. Get the key from his belt!"

I turned to look where she was pointing. As she said, there was a man asleep, hunched over a wooden desk. "Now!" she hissed.

"Where am I?" I asked.

"He will be back soon!"

I started to panic. "Who?"

"The other guard. Just get the key now!"

I tried to move, but I was shaking all over. My breath was fast and shallow, and every breath brought in another lungful of that awful smell. "I can't!" I protested.

"You have to!"

CHAPTER 22

I looked down at the book in my hand. It was dark, but I tried to read it anyway. I just couldn't handle this. I fled back to The Library.

Once I was sure that I was safe in my nook, I just sat there for a moment, my heart pounding.

Why was she shouting at me like that? Why did it smell so bad in there? That girl needed my help, and I didn't do anything. I ran away.

A cocktail of emotions swirled within me. Only Hank seemed to be fine with me running away, though he twitched his nose when I remembered how long I had been from detention. I took a deep breath and opened Alice.

Once I was back in the detention room, I saw that Darcy had returned. He was sitting a few rows in front of me, and it looked like he was reading the history book. I commanded my attention to the page, pushing away the experience I had just had in Elaine's book.

I wrote about half a page on one of the questions and then gave up and drew a dragon. This relaxed me. The dragon was curled up on a giant pile of books. A true treasure trove.

After about an hour, Mr. Wilson appeared again. "Where have you been?" he demanded of Darcy.

"Right here, Mr. Wilson. I just went to the toilet before. Is that allowed?"

"You know what really gets me?" asked Mr. Wilson, "how you can keep on messing up even though you know that it's just gonna be you and me here every Saturday until the end of time."

"It's just my character," said Darcy blankly.

"Most kids are like Miss Reed back there. They mess up once, they come in once, and I never see them on the weekend ever again."

Darcy whipped around and looked right at me. He looked afraid.

"Yes, Miss Reed. Although maybe you shouldn't stare at her like that."

Darcy held his gaze on me a moment longer, seeming to search my eyes. I looked away.

When I was finally out of that room, I did my best to make sure that I left school a different way than Darcy. I didn't like the way he looked at me. It got me worrying. Maybe he knew something was up with me? If his life was somehow tainted by the void, then I had to be more careful around him. Do I really want to freak him out?

If the wrong people found out about The Library, then they might try and take my book. I couldn't let that happen. I would have to be more careful about where I was when I went into The Library. If I disappeared and then reappeared right in front of people, then there would be questions.

After crossing the road from the front of the school, I glanced back for a moment. Darcy was standing by the school gates, was watching me leave.

Once I was clear from the school, I turned my phone back on. It immediately buzzed. I had received three messages while in detention, all of them from Mom.

Where are you?
We are taking Jonny to the fairy forest.
Talk later.

Shoot. I knew what talk later meant. Talk later meant I would be told how much I have messed up again. I would get that look, that one that said that she was disappointed in me. I hated that look.

I genuinely felt awful. When Jonny was talking about the fairies, I felt like I was nine again too. I just wanted to be transported back to that time where every tree log held secrets, and if you were quiet enough, you could hear the fairies singing.

The good kind of fairies.

Sorry, I was at Lilly's. Battery was flat.

It was a stupid excuse, and I knew it.

There is no way I wanted to go home now. Things were getting stressful, and I needed to talk to someone. Grandma volunteered at a thrift shop on Saturdays. Maybe I could catch her on her lunch break?

I always loved visiting my grandma's shop when I was a kid. It was always filled with the strangest looking mugs, ancient electronics, and hundreds of little glass ornaments. There were clothes there too. Some of them were nice, but most of them were so peculiar that you had to wonder how anyone bought them in the first place.

I waited for the bus at a stop some distance from school. Using the public transport system was always an adventure and one that Hank had a particular distaste for. I had a coping kit that I never failed to leave behind. This consisted of dark glasses, headphones, and my mobile or book.

I put on the glasses and plugged my headphones in. I wore the glasses even though it was cloudy. Similarly, I wore the headphones even when nothing was playing. I just had to block out the world. Though I was prepared, there was always the chance that someone would try and speak to me. I could feel Hank running around inside my stomach.

The bus pulled up.

Things had gotten more manageable now that you could just swipe a card to get on the bus. No worries about not having the right change or saying the wrong thing to a stressed bus driver. Just swipe and nod. Though, there was always the chance that the card would be empty.

I stepped onto the bus.

The bus driver was wearing dark glasses too. I wondered if we wore them for the same reasons. I scanned the bus for a place to sit. This was always tricky. If you sat next to someone, then they might think you want to talk. If you sit alone, then there was still the chance that someone at the next stop would sit next to you.

I took an empty seat near the back and pulled out my phone.

The journey seemed to be going well. Every time we

pulled up to a bus stop, Hank got a little excited, but that always passed when no one sat next to me.

Then the unthinkable happened.

"Hello again, dear."

It was the old lady from the bus stop across the road from the bookshop. She completely ignored my headphones. I made a mental note to get larger ones, maybe those enormous ones that covered your ears.

"Hi," I said.

My phone buzzed. Instinctively, I looked at it and inadvertently opened a message from Darcy. I winced with anxiety. I closed the message as fast as I could. What if the old lady saw it? What if she teased me about talking to a boy?

The world was a minefield.

"I think a storm is brewing," said the lady, peering out the window, "you wouldn't think it though, would you?"

"No," I said, "I like storms." I cringed. Was that even something people say?

"Oh, me too, dear. People always call it bad weather, but I like it."

"It's much better." I cringed again.

The worst thing about the conversation was that I was actually interested. Why couldn't Hank just leave me alone for five minutes? I just needed a rest.

Once off the bus, I read Darcy's message properly. I wasn't sure how he messaged me. I was only vaguely aware of how half the apps on my phone worked. Lilly kept putting new ones on to communicate in new and different ways. I guess Darcy must have been able to see me on one of them.

We need to talk.

CHAPTER 23

I read the message and then read it again. What did Darcy mean? Somewhere in the back of my mind, I was hearing warning bells about what boys do when they want to date you. I didn't think Darcy actually wanted to do that sort of thing. He was way too serious for that. But it still contributed to the soup of awkwardness.

This is why I don't go where people are.

I decided that I would handle the message the way I did best: by ignoring it and hoping it would go away. To be honest, I was kind of angry that he messaged me at all. It's not as though we were friends.

But then again, that would disqualify everyone in the world but Lilly, so there you go.

***

The musty smell of the thrift shop enveloped my experience. It was a friendly smell.

Behind the counter sat Agatha, Grandma's thrift shop friend. She never seemed to remember who I was, so I never said hello. I smiled at her, but her attention was on her magazine. It seemed Grandma was out to lunch.

I crept through the familiar shelves of second-hand treasures. Some of the items had been there since I was little. There was a creepy clown doll in the window, which I was fairly sure Grandma only kept as a joke. I loved the old jigsaw puzzles which no one bought, some of which I had completed with Grandma on rainy days. The whole place was a time capsule.

I wandered to the pre-loved books section, where my eyes scanned the shelves for Lewis Carroll. Some habits are hard to break. He wasn't there.

I sat down on an old creaky stool and picked out a book at random. Before long, I was enthralled by the description of an old house with a secret treasure.

"Hello, dear," said Grandma, pulling me back to the present.

"Grandma!" I said, jumping up and giving her a big hug.

"Would you like a cuppa?"

I nodded vigorously.

"It's lovely to see you," she said once we had sat down in the small kitchen out the back. "I do worry, with you being a teenager now, that you will lose interest in your old grandma."

"Of course not," I said, shaking my head. I wasn't that kind of teenager, and she knew it, but I guess even grandmas like to hear that their company is wanted.

Grandma always knew it was books and drawings, and the forests that were on my mind. She kind of got me in a way that no one else did, not even Lilly.

It was almost like we were related or something.

We talked about these things and others. The time flew by, and the tea drained away. It took me a while to build up to the question, but eventually, I asked it.

"Grandma, do you know what to do about anxiety?"

The question felt heavy and hung in the air for a moment.

She smiled kindly. "I have had my fair share of nerves over the years. They used to tease me about it, no end. They used to call me the wall garden."

"Wall garden?"

"Like a wallflower that takes its job more seriously."

I nodded and wondered who called her that.

"I was terrible," she continued, "couldn't speak to anyone I didn't already know, and even then, I fumbled over my words."

"Sounds familiar," I said.

"It's rough, dear. I know."

"But you got over it, right? You talk to the customers here all the time."

Grandma laughed. "No, dear. That's not quite how it works. I get nerves now just the same as ever I did."

"Really?" My heart sank. I was kind of banking on Hank taking a permanent holiday by the time I was Grandma's age.

"Don't look so solemn. I wouldn't get rid of my nerves even if I could."

"Why on earth not?"

"It's just your body's way of telling you that what you are doing is important, that's all. Once I realized I was nervous because I *wanted* to make friends, things got much easier. I started to see my nerves as a sort of a compass pointing me in the right direction. After all, if people weren't important to me, then why on earth would I care what they think?"

"I hate it."

"I know, dear. There is one way you could get rid of them, but it comes at a great cost."

"What's that? I'd do anything," I said, leaning forward in my seat.

"Never do anything important."

"Oh."

***

I stared out of the bus as the shops and people zipped by. I thought of all the things in my life that made me anxious and tried to match them up in my mind with all the things that I thought were important.

Something stirred deep inside me. Some old sadness that I didn't even know was there ached and throbbed. Tears welled up in my eyes.

I thought of all the things Hank had taken from me. I couldn't go places, I let people down, I couldn't be myself, I was perpetually in discomfort.

It wasn't supposed to be like this.

Pretty much everything in my life made me anxious. If Grandma was right, then I guess that had to mean that my life was very, very important to me. I had spent so much of my life running from anxiety, running, and hiding. Avoidance completely dominated me. Whenever Hank turned up, I just did whatever I could to get him to go again. I was a defective friend, a defective daughter, and a defective all-around human being.

There was a parallel dimension version of Alex, who didn't run from her feelings, and I was killing her every day. I was at a funeral, and it was the funeral for my own soul.

I got off the bus and wandered home. The house was empty. I collapsed on the couch, lying unmoving for quite a while.

Sometimes when I'm really upset, I just sort of freeze. Like, inside and out. I lie awake and just wait for time to be over. Sometimes I think that I don't really exist, or if I do exist that I don't have any free will. I imagine what it is like to not be able to move, and then I do that.

Today something different happened.

As I lay, a small fire kindled from somewhere in the depths of my heart. I thought about Mom, and I thought about the job she had tried to set up with Uncle Jack. She would be home soon. I was going to get told off for not being home for the day trip. At least I could do this one thing.

I got up from the couch and took a deep breath. I was going to do it. I was going to call my uncle and ask about the job.

I felt strange. There was a rush of power within me. I could feel Hank waking up inside me, but I didn't stop the feeling. I let it build.

For once, I was going to be in control of my life, not Hank.

I found Uncle Jack's number on a post-it note by the phone. Mom had left it to be found. I grabbed it, taking back control.

I might only have a few minutes. I picked up the house phone and began to dial. It felt strange holding a land-line telephone. I literally had no idea when I had last held one. The buttons were large and awkward and beeped as I entered each number.

I felt a rush of anticipation, my heart beating hard in my chest.

The phone rang once.

There was a thud.

The front door closed.

"Alex!" called Mom, "you home?"

CHAPTER 24

I froze for a moment, not knowing what to do.

I looked at the phone in my hand and pressed the button to hang up. As fast as I dared, I placed the phone back on its cradle. I ran upstairs to my room, dodging my parents as I did. The bedroom door closed behind me. I sat on the edge of the bed and closed my eyes.

My chance had passed me by.

I didn't want to stick around. I couldn't handle Mom today. I pulled out my phone and scrolled to Darcy's message.

OK, I typed in the reply box.

I hesitated, held my breath, and hit send.

Soon I was walking down the street toward Darcy's house. My hands and feet felt numb with anxiety. It was like I was watching myself walk from somewhere outside of my body.

I had known where Darcy lived for years now. It was information gleaned from social osmosis. It only took a few moments to walk there. I arrived at his house and was just about to step up to the front door and knock when I heard him call.

"Hey, over here!"

I turned about to see Darcy leaning out the window of a car across the road. I walked over.

"I'm not getting in a car with you," I said bluntly.

"It's private," he said.

"Do you even have your license?"

"Well, no, but we don't have to drive anywhere. Here, you can hold the keys." He pulled them out of the ignition and handed them to me.

"Fine, but please don't be a serial killer, OK?"

"Promise."

I climbed into his car and shut the door. It was the sort of car that people only ever drove because someone had given it to them. It smelled of stale cigarette smoke.

"OK, so what is this about?" I asked.

"It's about today in detention. You weren't in that room when I got back, and yet somehow, you were there when it was time to leave."

"I can just be really quiet sometimes," I said. I tried to make myself sound as honest as possible, but really, I suck at lying.

"You weren't there. I would have noticed."

"What, do you think that I was invisible? Come on."

"Were you?"

"What?"

"Were you invisible?"

"No."

"Look, I might need your help, but I need to know that I can trust you."

"Who says I wanna help?"

"Because there are lives at stake, and you are not a toer-ag."

An uneasy feeling stirred within me. I had known Darcy by sight for many years, and he never said so much as two words to me. Now he was acting all intense. My body seized up.

"I gotta go," I said.

"You are not serious."

"I am. Look, I was in the detention room the whole time, OK?"

"No, you weren't."

"Just leave me alone, would you?"

I popped open the car door.

"Fine!" he yelled after me.

As I walked home, my thoughts drifted to Lilly. Life was all too much for me to handle on my own. I had to tell her about The Library sooner or later. Why not tell her now?

Once home, I went straight upstairs, avoiding Mom.

I lay back on my bed and swiped the passcode into my phone. I just stared at the screen for a moment. What would I actually say to Lilly? It was all just too hard.

I placed the phone on my bedside table and opened Alice.

***

The cat was nowhere to be seen. It was another fine day out of the hanging window. The cat was probably out bounding through long grass or sleeping someplace in the sun.

Elaine's book was on the shelf where I left it. Taking a deep breath, I opened to the first chapter. Soon I was falling into the book. Loose pages fluttered and spun around me.

I landed on an earthen road.

A dense fog hung all about me. I was in some sort of town, but one unlike any I had seen before. The buildings towered, their walls made of rough-hewn stone, colonized by moss and vines. Wooden shutters were closed tight against the damp. The roofs were thatched and weather-worn.

It looked like I had gone back in time.

The street was dirty brown and littered with debris. There was an old wooden cart filled with hay leaning against the wall of a derelict house.

A noise drew my attention up the street. It sounded like people were running. They shouted as their steps clattered.

"Get out of sight!" someone hissed.

Startled, I spun around, looking for who had spoken.

"Here!" they said. There was a person underneath the hay cart, blending into the shadow.

"Elaine?"

"Get over here!"

I hurried over and crouched down next to her. Her black hair tumbled down her back, thick and wavy. She was wearing a rough cut black dress. A brown rucksack was slung over one shoulder.

She pulled me in close. It felt weird being so close to a stranger. The clatter of running feet came closer and closer.

Soon they were right upon us.

"Halt!" said a male voice, deep and gruff.

The clatter stopped.

Peering out through a gap in the cart, I could see that they were soldiers. There were about six of them standing there, alert. They were dressed in dull plate armor and looked like something out of a live-action roleplay convention. They were each carrying a long spear-like weapon and a wooden shield.

I tried to quiet my breathing. All was silent but for the steady drum of Elaine's heart.

"Alright, keep moving," said the voice.

The soldiers marched on.

After a moment, Elaine pushed me away and stepped out into the road.

"Who were they?" I asked.

"They are hunting me. We need to keep moving."

"Sure," I said.

"How did you know my name?" she asked as she led me down through the foggy streets.

"I just knew. I don't know." I didn't know what else to say.

"Psychic then? Well, I'm not. Who are you?"

"Alex."

"Interesting."

"Why?"

"Never mind. We have to get out of this city."

We hurried through the streets and had not gone far before Elaine pulled me against a wall. She looked about, eyes wide, and then hastened on.

Soon we came to an open area. There was a large body of water, a lake maybe. It was bordered by a cobbled path and a low wall. Fog concealed the far side.

All was silent, and no one was around.

"Is this place always so empty?" I asked.

"These days, yes. People have moved away from Avonheim since my sister disappeared." Elaine's eyes never seemed to stay still. She was as alert as a rabbit in an open field.

"Avonheim?"

"Yes. The Kingdom of Avonheim. My sister was its ruler, Lady Tabatha."

"What happened to her?"

"She was taken by the sorceress, Vicious. I need to get her back. Come, we mustn't linger."

We continued along the lakefront, staying low. My legs started to burn with fatigue.

"Where are we going?"

"We have to get to the city wall. There should be a boat waiting at the river moat."

"Can we stop a moment?" I asked.

"Why?"

"My legs."

"Really?" her tone was laced with sarcasm. "Ignore it."

She pulled me on. It seemed to me that she quickened her pace after that. She hurried down a narrow street, and I followed the best I could. My lungs were burning now.

"Hurry!" she said in a sharp whisper.

"I," gasp, "can't."

"I see 'em!" bellowed a voice.

We both spun around to see a tall figure up the road behind us, pointing our way. A sea of spears gathered behind him.

CHAPTER 25

The soldiers didn't wait long. Soon they were hurtling toward us at an alarming rate. "Now, can you run?" hissed Elaine, grabbing my arm.

And run I did, dodging discarded carts and abandoned market stalls.

We continued down the road for a time, the soldiers gaining on us. We ducked down a lane, out onto another street, and then down another alley. The whole city was a maze, a ghost town of stone and fog.

The guards clattered behind us. Somehow they were still gaining on us, even as we weaved. "We are almost there," called Elaine over her shoulder.

We came to a wall. It was tall enough for its height to be concealed by the fog. Elaine lifted aside a crude wooden door behind which was a tunnel. We plunged into the darkness.

There was a faint light ahead. I couldn't see where my feet were landing. There were pools of water on the ground, and soon my shoes were soaked through.

Behind us, the soldiers found the tunnel entrance. Their shouts bounced and echoed all around.

As we got closer to the end of the tunnel, it became apparent that there was a figure there, waiting for us. Its eyes glowed faintly in the darkness. Elaine seemed unconcerned. When we reached the figure, I found that it was enormous, towering over us by several feet. It stepped aside and allowed us to pass.

A small wooden boat bobbed gently in the shallows of a river. Mangrove shoots speckled the mud.

"Get in," said Elaine.

My feet sank and squelched in the mud. I held the side of the boat down and scrambled in, pulling in half the river as I did. Elaine followed with significantly more grace. She seized the oars and started to row.

I looked back toward the tunnel. The towering figure had stepped back in place, blocking the tunnel exit.

The fog swirled around us.

"Will they be OK?" I asked.

"Who? Oh, the big guy? Yeah, he can look after himself."

There was a scream and a shout. Through the fog, I could just make out movement, but could not see what was happening. There was a loud splash as something substantial plunged into the water.

Elaine paddled on.

Soon the sounds of the skirmish faded, and we were nearing the opposite side of the river moat.

Once we were out of the boat, I took off my shoes and spilled out the water and mud. This would probably take quite a bit of explaining to Mom.

"We should be safe here for a moment," said Elaine,

collapsing onto the stony shore.

"The fog?"

"Yeah. It's a mixed bag for the citadel."

"It seems strange to me," I said.

"It's a curse."

"It's not so bad."

"I mean a literal curse. The council placed it on the citadel to prevent the goblin raids. It worked for a while too."

"Goblin raids?"

"Yeah, vicious creatures. These hills are swarming with them. You will find that most of the villages in these parts are either walled or empty."

I peered suspiciously at the woods that hung all around.

"I wouldn't let them worry you."

"How come?"

"I dearly love killing goblins."

"Oh."

"Look," she sat up, "I am going to need your help getting my sister back."

"My help? I don't know what I can do."

"Before I was imprisoned by the idiots in there, I heard a prophecy that a phantom would help me get Tabatha back before it was too late."

"You think I'm a phantom?"

"Please. You appear and disappear at random. You dress in strange clothes. You don't seem to know where you are. What else would you call that?"

"Maybe I'm a ghost."

She picked up a stone and threw it at me. It struck my arm. "Ouch," I said. It stung.

"Not a ghost. Now, will you help me?"

I looked at the ground, dodging her gaze.

"My sister was the ruler in these lands. She had special powers that helped keep the peace. I was there when the sorceress Vicious transformed her into a bird and stole her away."

"Like, a literal bird?"

"Yes, and it was dreadful. I went after her but lost the trail. When I went back to the citadel to see if there was anything that would indicate where they had gone, I was seized by the commander of the city watch. He is convinced that I am responsible for the disappearance of Lady Tabatha. It is exceedingly frustrating. As annoying as this was, the set back did lead me to discover the sorceresses trail. She has taken refuge in the Hollow Hills."

"I don't think I will be much help."

"That may be so, but I am not one to ignore prophecy. Just help me get my sister back before it's too late. If we don't get to her soon, then she may well be eaten. Vicious is like that."

"That's dreadful!"

"So, will you come along, or what?"

CHAPTER 26

I emerged from Elaine's story to find the cat staring at me with steady eyes. I closed the book and looked at it, tracing my finger over the face embossed on the cover, trying to figure out what I should do. I thought of the two little girls who had been cast out of their village.

I wanted to help them.

Could Elaine be trusted? She was a little rough around the edges, to be sure. One thing was for certain, I didn't want to be the person who judged her before I knew her.

Who knows, maybe I could be of some help?

I didn't see my family until the next morning. When I came down for breakfast, I could feel the tension in the air. There was a storm brewing, and it could hit at any moment.

"We went to the fairy forest yesterday," said Jonny as he eagerly shoveled an oversized piece of pancake into his mouth.

"I know you did," I said, "did you see any sign of the fairies?"

"Yup. I found the table where they sit, and I found one of the mushroom houses. I wanted to take one home so that they could live in my room, but Dad said they are poisonous."

"Probably best that they live in their own forest anyway," I said.

"Yeah, probably."

"You would have enjoyed it," said Mom in a steady and calculated tone.

"Next time I'll be there for sure," I said to Jonny, trying to avoid Mom's gaze.

"You missed out!" shouted Dad from his position in front of the TV, "we went to the Buffet House for lunch."

"Oh," I said. My heart sank. We never went out anywhere for food. Did they go without me to deliberately make me feel left out? It stung.

"Look at this mess," said Mom to Jonny. Jonny grinned back, proud of his work. "Why don't you go upstairs and clean yourself up?"

"OK," said Jonny. He jumped up and bolted away, stomping his feet with every step with pure, unmediated enthusiasm.

I braced myself.

"You really need to let us know when you are going to Lilly's," said Mom sternly.

"I know, I'm sorry. My phone died."

Mom was looking at me with the same look Mrs. Taylor gave me when I didn't have my speech prepared. I just wanted to shrink into nothingness.

"You could have let me know before, or borrowed a phone. We were waiting for you. You know that, right?"

"I know."

"So you can't do that, Alex. It's no way to treat people. You are almost an adult, and if you continue down this selfish path, then you are not going to have anyone in your life who will stick by you."

"Mom," I stammered. My heart was pounding now, and I felt sick. My lip quivered.

"I don't want to see the tears, Alex. Poor Jonny was so disappointed. He just wanted to spend time with his big sister."

"I wanted to go," I said desperately.

"Not badly enough, obviously! And have you given your uncle a call?"

I tried to will the tears away but to no avail.

"I went through a lot of trouble setting that up. All you needed to do was call him. He will be very disappointed that he hasn't heard from you. Opportunities like that don't come along all the time, especially in today's job market."

I couldn't stand there anymore. I just couldn't. I turned my back and started walking up the stairs.

"You can't run away from everything," she called after me.

I slammed the door as hard as I could. It bounced off of a sweater on the floor. I moved it aside and slammed the door again. This time, there was a satisfying crash.

How could she think so poorly of me? I did my best! I didn't ask for detention, and I didn't ask her to find me a job. It was all so stupid.

I plunged my face into my sheets and let the tears flow.

After a while, my phone buzzed. I ignored it for a moment, preferring to pretend I was a pillow. It was probably Lilly. I unlocked the phone with a swift swipe.

Meet at mine before the movie? Starts at 2:45. Mine at 2?

There was no way I could face this today.

I can't come.

I turned off my phone's screen and grabbed for Alice. At least I had one place where I could be alone.

Alice was beginning to get very tired...

CHAPTER 27

I landed on a damp forest floor. The weave of the trees overhead was dense, and very little light penetrated to the stunted canopy below. Looking about, I could see that I was halfway up a hill. A lively waterfall fed a small pool at the foot of a steep bank.

A figure was bent over in the shallows. They appeared to be washing something in the water, occasionally pausing to check their progress before continuing to scrub.

They turned suddenly, locking eyes with me.

"Oh, it's you," they said. It was Elaine.

I approached. As I did, she squeezed the water out of the garment she was cleaning. Black as it was, it stained the shallow water pink.

"What's wrong?" she asked when I reached her.

"I guess my face looks puffier than I thought."

"Looks like you have had a run-in with a poisoned vine." She cocked her head and examined me closely.

"Nah, just drama. Never mind. What's happening with you?"

She gestured to a crude bandage around her left arm.

"Oh, no. What happened?"

"Goblins. They attacked a village to the south of here. I

tried to fend them off, but they sacked it."

"That's awful."

Elaine shrugged. "Only if you happened to live there."

"We don't have goblins where I'm from."

"Lucky for you then."

"I guess."

There was a brief silence as I thought about what it must have been like for the poor people in the village. Elaine was unconcerned.

"Wanna do something cool?" she asked.

Elaine led me down the valley and through the dense forest. I had never seen a place as wild anywhere before. The forest was alive with sounds. Mostly, I heard bird-life singing strange melodies, but there were also numerous insect sounds too, punctuated by an occasional frog.

Now and then, a butterfly flew over our path, delicate and beautiful, with surreal colorings of blue and purple. Elaine didn't seem to notice them.

I could have wandered there for hours.

After a time, the trees thinned, and sunlight started to shine onto the undergrowth.

The more we walked, the more tall grasses and rough shrubs dominated. The ground slowly became damp and turned to mud.

There was a vague path through the bog, but it was frequently flooded, giving us no choice but to wade through the muck.

Elaine didn't say much as we walked, but every now and then, she sang a line or two of a song. It was both strange and familiar.

At last, we came to a stop. We were right on the edge of the forest now.

"Are you ready to see something extraordinary?"

"This whole place is amazing."

"Well, this is even better."

Another few steps and we were through the trees. The world opened up into a vast field. Though the view was breathtaking, my attention was drawn toward the giant duck immediately in front of us.

"His name is Pickles," said Elaine, proud.

Pickles quacked in recognition, loud and deep. Attached to his beak was a harness. A saddle was fixed to his back.

"What is that?" I asked in disbelief. It seemed so real.

It was real.

"He's a duck. You don't have ducks where you are from?"

"We do, but they are not usually so large."

"This guy is a bit unique. Come on, let's go for a ride."

"Wait, what? On a duck?"

"Sure, why not?" She pulled herself up onto the saddle and patted the space behind her. Pickles swayed a little under her weight. He shook his tail feathers and quacked again.

Hank cleared his throat and listed all the reasons why it was a bad idea to ride a duck. I was torn between fear of riding him and fear of looking like a dork in front of Elaine. I climbed up, and Elaine took my hand, pulling me onto the saddle.

Pickles started to waddle. I felt him sway beneath

me. Every step seemed like it would be the one to send us plummeting to the grassy ground below. I gripped Elaine's clothes tightly to keep from falling off.

"Pretty fun, huh?" Elaine said over her shoulder.

"Just focus on where you are going," I said urgently.

"Don't worry," said Elaine, "it's not as though we have even taken off yet."

"Taken off?!"

I hardly had time to freak out before Pickles extended his wings and started beating them hard. It seemed ridiculous that something this large could fly, but all the same, my heart was hammering double-time.

"Hold on!" Elaine called out. Pickles was running now, faster, and faster. His wings were flapping harder and harder. Then suddenly, impossibly, Pickles took flight.

My stomach turned as we lurched upward.

Everything was chaos. Feathers and wings thudded all around me. I squeezed my eyes shut and blocked out the world.

Pickles seemed to steady. The flapping fit was replaced with gentle gliding and the occasional purposeful beat of impossible wings. I squinted open my eyes, focusing on the horizon.

"Is this safe?" I yelled over the wind.

"I hope not!" called back Elaine. She laughed. The sound was caught by the wind and carried away.

I tried to focus on something in the distance. A mountain range caught my eye. It rose in a tremendous snow-capped arch out of the ground. It was magnificent.

I breathed deeply and started to feel steady.

"I'm taking him down to swoop," called Elaine.

My eyes widened involuntarily. Panic shot through my nervous system as Hank clawed at every switch and lever he could reach.

I closed my eyes and held my breath. Pickles dived toward the ground. The force against me was strong now. I was convinced I was going to fall off. My mind spun.

I thought of the book in my side bag and wondered if I could open it on the right page in time before hitting the ground. I pictured Alice spinning out of my hands as I fell to my death.

The ground rushed up fast.

Goodbye, world.

Elaine pulled hard on the duck's reins. Pickles honked and thudded his wings desperately. We were ascending into the sky again.

"Whoa!" she screamed.

I couldn't scream. I couldn't move. I think Elaine must have noticed because soon Pickles was steady again, and we were slowly descending towards an open patch of dirt by the bank of a winding river.

With a few pounding flaps, Pickles landed us gently on the solid ground.

I tried to climb down, but my body was too shaky with adrenaline. I fell onto the dirt, and pain shot up through my left wrist. I rolled over and cradled it, my heart pounding.

Elaine elegantly dismounted. She looked briefly at the way I was holding my hand and then turned away as if this was an inconvenience she was choosing not to acknowledge.

"I think it grows somewhere by this river bend," she said, leading the duck.

"What does?"

"You will see."

I closed my eyes and tried to process what had just happened.

"You coming?" called Elaine from some distance.

I was shaking as I stood up. One step at a time, I followed her toward the river. I watched as Elaine bent down and pulled up a plant. It was a wildflower with tiny deep crimson petals. She seemed satisfied with what she had and stuffed it into her bag.

"See if you can find more like this," she said, holding up one of the flowers for me to see.

I nodded and crouched down to begin the search. The activity seemed strangely docile after our aerial expedition. I stuffed several of the plants into my bag and then rested against a rock. The river tumbled along.

By now, it was late afternoon, and I was exhausted. For a brief moment, I remembered the date I was supposed to be on with Lilly. The pang stung straight to my heart. I inhaled sharply, pushing that thought away.

When Elaine was done picking the flowers, she joined me.

"I'm guessing that you have had enough duck for one day?"

"It was kind of terrifying."

"You did well, though, for your first time."

My heart swelled with gratitude at the compliment,

but I said nothing.

Elaine led Pickles along the river for a while. The land-scape turned from field to marsh, and pretty soon, we were once more dodging the mud.

"Where are we going?" I asked. My feet were getting tired, but I didn't want to go back to my world, not yet.

"We are going here," said Elaine, "look."

She pointed to a reed that was growing by the side of the river. At the top of the stalk, there was a fluffy white mass. "It couldn't be," I said, smiling.

"A marshmallow," said Elaine, "I take it you have those where you are from?"

"Yeah, except they make them out of boiled bones and sugar."

"Bones? That sounds way more interesting."

"These look much better."

We gathered up the marshmallows as the afternoon crept on. When we were done, Elaine tied the duck's harness to a tree some distance inland and started a small campfire by the river. The sun was beginning to set now, casting a reddish glow over the horizon. It all felt pretty special.

I had not had roasted marshmallows since I was little. The sticky sweet mass filled my experience. Even though they came from a random plant by the river, they still tasted exactly as I remembered.

Elaine produced a small cauldron from her backpack, filled it with water from the river, and settled it among the hot embers of the fire. Gradually, whisps of steam started dancing over the water's surface. These gave way to bubbles as the water boiled. Once the water was steaming steadily, Elaine carefully removed the cauldron from the fire and began dropping in a few of the petals and leaves from her stash of flowers.

"What are you making?" I asked.

"Tea," she said.

After a few minutes, she served the tea into two clay mugs and handed one to me.

"Thanks," I said, gazing into the warm liquid.

"Why don't you take a sip?"

CHAPTER 28

It just looked like herbal tea, like chamomile, maybe. It smelled vaguely of cherries and licorice. I felt uneasy but didn't want to be the awkward one.

I took a sip.

Elaine was watching me closely, nodding and smiling as I drank. For a moment, I thought that maybe she was poisoning me, and I was allowing her to do so because I wanted to be polite.

To my relief, Elaine blew on her tea and began to drink too.

In the shadows, a curious fox crept up to share the warmth of the fire.

"Watch this," she said, turning to face the fire. She started to wave her hands slowly, moving them as if she were molding the air.

At first, it appeared that she was just messing around, but then the flames began to change.

A trick of the eye? No, the changes were unmistakable. A flower was blooming among the flames, delicate and shimmering.

"How did you do that?" I asked, astonished.

"It's the tea," said Elaine, smiling.

"How?"

"It allows me to tap into a fire realm slightly beyond this reality. It's like it helps to tilt your mind to a certain angle for a little while. Why don't you give it a try?"

Hesitating, I raised my hands. It all felt very silly.

I pictured what I wanted to form in the flames. I imagined one of the lilac butterflies I had seen in the forest earlier. I pictured it as I would have if I were drawing on my tablet.

And then, as we watched, the flames morphed and changed. From somewhere deep within the embers, a butterfly, my butterfly, unfolded its wings and fluttered up to Elaine's flower, landing gently on a petal.

Elaine's jaw dropped. "I'm impressed!" she said.

"I do a lot of drawing," I said, apologetically.

"I don't know what that means, but you seem to have a talent. I've never seen anyone create anything on the first go."

"Thanks."

"You sure you haven't done this before?"

I nodded.

Elaine then started to form another shape. The flower changed. Each of its petals elongated and then bent into eight spindly legs. The spider pounced at my butterfly. The butterfly dodged and then flew away, disappearing into the night.

I thought of the fox at the edge of the fire and started to shape its likeness. First, its curious black eyes formed in the flames, followed by its face and its twitching ears. Soon, its whole body sat squatting in the campfire. Its face was full of expression.

I found that I could make him move. He chased his tail and tried to howl, but all that could be heard was the crackle of the fire.

"Oh yeah?" said Elaine, "take this." From within the flames, an indistinct shape emerged, it might have been a tiger or a leopard, but its form was uneven as if a child had drawn it - a child with nightmares. It shimmered and shook in the heat. With a swift gesture from Elaine, it pounced on my fox, crushing it, sending sparks and ash flying. The creature opened its mouth to roar and revealed impossible rows of triangular teeth.

Elaine looked over to the real fox on the edge of the firelight. A sly smile crept over her face. With a swift flick of her hand, the half-formed beast bounded at the fox.

"Elaine, no!" I cried, but it was too late. The flames were upon the fox. It yelped in pain and then bounded into the night.

Elaine fell over backward, laughing.

"Why on earth did you do that?"

"Same reason I do anything, Miss Serious. For fun. Why? What does it matter?"

"The poor guy is hurt," I said. I imagined what it must be like for the fox, alone, confused, and in pain.

"It's just a dumb animal," said Elaine, defensively.

"It can still feel pain."

"Jeeze, way to be a killjoy, Alex."

I didn't say anything to that.

We sat in silence for a while. Elaine roasted up another marshmallow and then picked at it. At length, she looked up at me.

"So when are you going to leave anyway?" she asked.

"Dunno," I said honestly. I didn't much want to hang out with Elaine at this point, but going home didn't seem like the best idea either.

"I'm sorry about the fox," she said, "I didn't know you would be bothered by it. People around here don't think much of foxes. They mostly see them as chicken thieves."

"Forget about it," I said, more because that's the sort of thing you are supposed to say in these situations than because I meant it.

Part of me wanted to just gloss over the situation because I didn't want to make this place just another place I avoided. I mean, Elaine was looking for her lost sister, and that was pretty important. And the book had called me, at least I think it had called me, and that was pretty important too.

Elaine could one day end up like the old woman I saw in The Library, and maybe I was the only one who could prevent that.

I wanted to go home to a quiet house with everyone in bed. I just couldn't face them today. When the moon had risen a fair way into the sky, I stood up.

"Leaving?" asked Elaine. She almost sounded disappointed, which was weird. It's not a though we were talking.

"Yeah, I gotta get some sleep."

"Why not sleep here?"

"Maybe another time. Thanks for everything. That duck was cool, scary, but cool."

"Hey, no problem."

I opened up Elaine's book and began to read. I was conscious that Elaine's eyes were on me. I glanced up at her just before falling into the book. She met my gaze for a moment and then looked away.

I landed in The Library in a crouch. I stood up and was about to pick up Alice when a thought struck me.

I opened Elaine's book again and fell back into her world. As I hoped, I landed some distance from the circle of the fire. I crept forward through the darkness.

The stars overhead filled the sky in a way that I never saw back home.

Pickles was sat on the ground in a huddle. It seemed like he was sleeping. I found the tree which his harness was tied to and felt for the knot. I fumbled with it for a few moments, and it began to loosen.

The rope dropped to the ground with a thud. Pickles' eyes flickered open. "Nice duck," I said, "now let me take off that harness."

Pickles quacked.

"Shhhh. Just let me-"

He quacked again and stood up, ruffling his feathers.

"Now just hold still."

Pickles began to run. For a moment, I thought about running after him. I wanted to take off that harness so he could be properly free, but it was too late. I shrugged in the darkness.

He was free enough.

It was after midnight when I was finally back in my room. I was as tired as I have ever been.

The notification light on my phone winked at me,

accusingly. A pang of guilt shot up from somewhere in my gut and careered right into my heart. I turned on my phone's screen.

There were 10 unread messages, all from Lilly.

CHAPTER 29

"Shoot," I hissed.

I'm really sorry.

I sent the message without reading any of Lilly's messages. I just couldn't handle them tonight, but I needed to know that she was OK. I lay down on my bed, gripping my phone tightly, hoping that Lilly wasn't angry with me and wishing that things had gone differently.

Sleep took me.

As soon as I was awake, I grabbed for my phone and swiped it unlocked.

Nothing.

I thought for a moment about reading Lilly's messages, just in case there was something in them that would let me know how angry she was with me, but I couldn't do it. I just wanted everything to be OK.

No Lilly was waiting for me at the front gates of the school, either. I waited right up until the bell rang, just in case she was running late, but she was nowhere to be seen.

I had really screwed up this time.

All through my morning classes, my mind whirred with a thousand different ways in which I could apologize, a thousand ways in which I could make it up to her.

I couldn't concentrate.

At lunchtime, I saw Lilly from across the courtyard. She saw me, but then pointedly turned away and sat with some of her other friends. She always had other friends, she was just that kind of person. I sat alone with my lunch and my phone.

Once I had built up the courage, I opened her messages and began to read. It was painful. After my text saying that I couldn't come, her first reply was full of concern and encouragement. Her care made me ache when contrasted to the look she had just given me. I kept reading and somewhere between the *hun*? and *hello*? it seemed that she had gotten mad. The last few were the most painful as she started saying what she really felt, culminating with:

If you can't even be bothered messaging me back, then I don't know that we should bother being friends! It's clearly too much of an inconvenience!

I sat alone all lunch. I couldn't read, I didn't want to go into The Library, I couldn't really do anything. I just sat, absorbing time as it went by. The sky was changing, becoming charged as it does before a storm. Ordinarily, I would have loved that. Today I didn't care.

Lilly was in all my classes after lunch, but she persisted in avoiding my gaze. I just wanted her to understand that I didn't flake on the date to hurt her, I wanted her to understand that I just couldn't handle it. I wanted her to shake her head at me as she always did with my weird ways and just say: 'you're a worry, Alex.'

I couldn't even get her to talk to me.

There was only one thing I could do to make it up to her. I would have to take her to The Library. There was no way she could stay angry at me once she had seen what I had seen.

Determination swelled in my chest, and my dull mood gave way to excitement over my decision. All I needed to do was talk to her alone. I would say sorry and then show her the book. Everything was going to be OK.

After school, Lilly left class quickly. I followed after her best I could but lost her in the hoards of students. I caught sight of her heading to the exit at the back of the field.

I hurried after her.

She was already halfway across the grass now, a black figure against a field of green.

"Lilly!" I called.

She didn't stop but kept on marching towards the bank of trees on the far side. I quickened my pace and then started to run. Somewhere in the distance, thunder cracked. Soon the field would be a swamp.

"Lilly, I'm sorry!"

She stopped walking and turned around. She had a bitter expression. It seemed strange on her usually sunny face. It stung me to the core.

"What are you doing here, Alex?"

"Lilly, I'm sorry. I messed up."

"Yeah, you messed up," she said flatly.

"I was having an awful day," I said, feeling stupid even as the words escaped my lips.

"So you thought you would share it around? What's your deal, Alex? I mean, I get that things are hard for you sometimes, but I don't get how you can be such a horrible friend."

"My anxiety. You don't know what it's like."

"I'm a human being, Alex! Of course I know what it's like. Do you think you are the only one who gets it? Like you are somehow special? You aren't."

"Hey," I said, anger flaring up inside.

"I was super anxious yesterday, Alex. I needed my friend with me to support me, but instead of being able to look after myself I had to look after you, coax you out, try and convince you not to hurt me. I don't need that in my life."

"I didn't ask you to."

"You never do! You just wait around for people to come to your rescue. Well, I'm done being your hero. Find someone else to carry you."

My face contorted, and my eyes welled with tears.

"Save it," said Lilly, coldly. "I'm not going to comfort you when *you* are the one that hurt *me*."

I couldn't take the way she was looking at me like I was worthless. I turned and started to run for the school. As I did, the rain poured.

CHAPTER 30

I needed to get away now. Once inside the school, I pulled out Alice and read the first line, heedless of where I was.

I left a trail of footprints as I walked through The Library. All I wanted was to jump into one of these books and never come back. No one would miss me.

Lilly was supposed to be the one person that understood me, the one person who could put up with my weirdness. I shook my head. She was just like all the others, after all. She told me that she liked me and didn't find me annoying while secretly she was getting more and more frustrated with me every day.

I looked about The Library for the fireplace, half-blind with tears and rage and sorrow.

The sound of fast footfall on the tiled ground made me pause. I turned around to see an eight-foot gorilla galloping towards me.

"Alex," she said, catching her breath, "you mustn't go into a book like that."

I looked down at my wet clothes and back up at the Librarian. "I'm looking for the fireplace to dry them," I sobbed.

"Not the clothes Alex, with a mood that strong. The books are sensitive, you know. If you enter a story with a mood as foul as yours, you risk putting yourself and others in great danger."

"My mood is fine," I barked.

The Librarian smiled a knowing smile. "I am a librarian, Alex. You cannot fool a librarian."

"So, what am I supposed to do?"

"Do whatever you need to feel better, just don't go into a book."

"But books are how I feel better!" I protested.

"Then you are going to have to find some new ways. That is unless you want to die."

"Alright!" I said.

Being called out on my mood made me feel even worse. I found the fireplace and took off my jacket and socks. The rest would just have to dry on me.

I curled up and tried not to exist.

I lay there for quite some time, listening to the distant tick of a clock, and watching the fire dance. At length, I decided that I was calm enough to enter a book.

I found Elaine's book and soon felt myself being sucked inside.

I landed in the middle of a sparse pine forest. Sunlight was poking through the canopy. The ground was uneven but easily walkable. The distinct scent of pine filled my awareness and reminded me distantly of Christmas.

Somewhere out of sight, a stream burbled on.

Elaine was nowhere to be seen. This was strange, but

I didn't much care, I didn't exactly feel like talking to anyone.

Now that I was on my feet, my mind just kept spinning back to Lilly and how unfair she was being. It's not my fault that I feel anxiety like I do.

Sure, I felt stink thinking that maybe she felt it too, and I wasn't there for her, but I was just so used to her being the confident one that it seemed ridiculous to think that anything about our inner worlds could really be the same.

I screamed at a nearby tree, feeling childish as soon as the noise escaped me.

The world shook, and I fell to the ground.

I landed in the soft pine needles. A pinecone prevented the fall from being painless. I sat up, eyes wide.

Did I just cause an earthquake?

"Damn it!" shouted a voice from somewhere nearby. I looked up in the direction of the voice. It was a male voice and sounded upset. I hesitated and then walked toward the sound.

There, getting to his feet and dusting himself off was a man. He was short, bald, and wore a black and white checkered coat. His shoes had bells on the end.

"I'm sorry, did I frighten you?" I asked, cautiously.

"Frighten me, sa? Yes, sa. Thought it was a dragon, sa. I'm quite relieved to see that you are just a girl, sa, pardon me for saying."

"That's OK. I'm Alex."

"Pleasure to meet you, Alex. I'm Mason, aren't I."

"I don't know, are you?

"Ah, yes, sa."

"Where are we, Mason?"

"Deep in the deep forest, sa. I am on a sacred errand, you see. A quest! I am journeying over field and fountain, and, er..."

"And what?"

"And lakes, sa. There was a lake back yonder, actually. Have to say I liked the field the best, sa. But who's keeping score?"

"You are, apparently."

"Until the day I die, sa."

"What is your quest?"

"A grave one indeed, sa. I was charged with a sacred duty, sa. And I have every intent on following it through, sa!"

"Why do you keep saying 'sa'?"

He looked puzzled for a moment. "Didn't realize I was saying that out loud. I'll say it in my head from now on." He adjusted his hat, "well, you see, s-, well, you see, I was in the employ of Lady Tabatha."

He puffed himself up with importance.

"Lady Tabatha?"

Mason started to tear up. "I'm sorry, it makes me sad just thinking about what happened."

"Well, I don't want to make you sad."

"I couldn't really get sadder, you know. Sad as sad. Just thinking about her, beak, feather, and claw. I don't care. She was a real lady."

"Apart from the beak?"

"She never used to have a beak. Not until recently. If she did, then I'm sure she kept it well hidden. Lips are all ever I saw. No, she was turned into a parrot."

"A parrot?"

"Beautiful, actually, red and green. Lovely plumage."

"Oh."

"So sad. Was the sorceress Vicious who done it. Always jealous of her power, she was. That's where I'm headed now, actually. I'm going to perform a daring rescue."

"Do you have much experience in daring rescues?"

"Not strictly speaking, no. I do have a wooden sword, though. Want to see me flourish?"

"If that is something that you do with your sword, then go ahead."

"Alright, watch this," he drew a tattered wooden sword from a cloth sheath at his belt. He lost his grip on the handle, and it flew off into a bush. "Right, whoops. Yes, that does happen. I'll just go get that. He waddled off into the undergrowth, his enormous shoes flapping, the bells on his toes chiming.

"It's a long way to her lair," he said as he stumbled back onto the path. The effort had him gasping for breath, "so I'll have plenty of time to practice drawing my sword."

"What exactly did you do for Lady Tabatha before she was, er, transformed?"

"Made a fool of myself, mostly."

"You are a fool?"

"I'm no one's fool!" he said, his mouth wide with shock, "but I am a jester."

"Of course, sorry. Well, Vicious sounds quite dangerous. Are you sure you aren't better off leaving the rescue to someone with a real sword?"

"She was always kind to me, sa, and the citadel ain't going to send anyone off to find her. They said I'd be a fool to try. I had to tell 'em that I would be a jester to try. I'm always correcting people."

He was resolute. Fortunately for him, it didn't seem like he was at all capable of going on a long journey. It was likely that Elaine would get to the Hollow Hills long before this strange man.

Elaine had an aura of capability about her, which made me think that she at least had a chance against the sorceress. If anyone read Mason's aura, then it was probably saying that he better stick with inside jobs.

"Well, I must be off, sa. The road ahead is dangerous."

"Good luck!"

"A pleasure to have conversed with you. Do you mind if I make a personal remark, sa?"

"O...K..."

"It's nothing bad or nothing, just, Lady Tabatha. You remind me a little of her."

"Thank you."

"Highest form of praise I know. Well, farewell." He bowed awkwardly, spun around, and fell over.

CHAPTER 31

Gingerly, Mason got to his feet and waddle-marched down the track and through the pines. When he was down a little way, he started singing, "da-da da-da-da." It sounded exactly like one of the songs from the Lord of the Rings movies.

I was wandering among the trees for a while before I came upon Elaine. She was standing with her back to a rather broad tree. I startled her.

"Are you OK?" I asked.

"What? Yeah, yeah, I'm fine. What's up with you? Have a swim?"

I looked down at my shirt. It was still wet from the rain at school. I guess it was odd to see someone soaking wet on such a fine day.

"It's raining back home."

"Strange."

"Hey, I ran into someone else looking for your sister. Did you know that others were trying to rescue her?"

"People will do anything for a reward."

"I don't think he was the type."

Elaine shrugged. "Well, my sister will be food for the

sorceress if we don't get to her soon."

"That's so gross."

"At least she turns people into animals before she eats them."

"That's supposed to make it better?"

"It is a little better."

"No, it's not."

"Fine, whatever. Well, we are going to need to pick up our pace now. That duck wandered off after you left. We will have to walk the rest of the way."

"Oh, dear. Is it far?"

"Not too far."

Elaine led me along a trail through the woods. She seemed to know her way around pretty well. Our path climbed up a ridge for a time, and the cover changed from pine to an eclectic array of trees I couldn't name. The undergrowth grew thick.

After a while, I could hear the sound of a strong river ahead. As we got closer, it roared.

"Will we be crossing that river?" I asked. I was a little worried that I might actually have to swim after all.

"Sure will. Don't worry, there is a bridge."

We walked a little further. After a time, Elaine held up her hand for me to stop. She crouched.

"See him there?" she pointed to a man standing by the bridge on our side.

"Yeah, I see him."

"We need to get past him in order to cross."

"Do we pay him?" I asked.

"Yeah, but I'm going to need your help with this one."

"Me?" My heart skipped a beat.

"Don't look so terrified. I just need you to do the talking, that's all."

"That's all?!"

"Well, you remember how I was in a prison cell when you met me."

"Vaguely."

"And all those men who chased us through the city?"

"I remember something like that."

"Well, they all still think I'm responsible for my sister's disappearance. I'll need you to do the talking. If he recognizes me, we could both be in big trouble. Once we are over and in the next county, I shouldn't have any problems. People don't know me there."

Hank started to list all the ways I would mess this up. My stomach flipped and flopped. I didn't want to move.

"I'll have to cover my face, but that shouldn't be a problem. That way, he will probably think I'm a nun."

"But if your face is covered, why can't you do the talking?"

"Um, cos I'm a nun? Nuns don't speak."

I was about to protest that they did where I was from, but that was pointless.

"So, you will do it then?"

"Sure," I squeaked, amazed at the word coming out of my mouth.

Elaine handed me two silver coins and covered her face with a black cloth.

When it was time to walk out toward the toll-person, my body froze. Every instinct was telling me to stay where

I was, escape into the book, run away, anything but talk to the human.

I stepped out into the open.

I could feel the man's eyes on me, wondering who I was and what I wanted. Here I am, just Alex, a normal human being walking with my friend, the nun. Don't mind me, I'm just being normal.

"Why are you walking like that?" hissed Elaine.

"Like what?"

"Shh."

"Hello, miss," said the man. His accent was thick, as were his shoulders. His arms were like tree trunks, and he held a spear.

"Hello, sir," I said. I just said sir. Was that even right? Does he think I'm weird?

"One silver for your passage over the bridge."

I handed him the two that Elaine gave me. I mean, she must have given me two for a reason, right? The guard looked at the coins and then back at me.

Awkwardness careered through my body. I turned into a little worm, ready to crawl away.

"You are very kind," said the man and gestured for me to pass.

We inched onto the wooden bridge. It was a rickety old thing, the sort I wouldn't dare cross in my own world, but right then, I didn't care.

I had managed to pass the human.

Far below us, the rapidly running river churned and rumbled.

I walked like I was an inch taller. A feeling of elation

flooded my chest. Elaine had asked me to do something, and I did it. I didn't run, I just did it.

Take that, Hank!

"Did you see that?" I asked excitedly when we were on the other side.

"Yeah, thanks for that."

"I totally talked to the man, and it was all fine."

"Yea...?" said Elaine, puzzled.

"You don't understand, I can't do that sort of thing. It was like magic!"

"That's what you call magic in your world?"

"In my world, things like that don't happen."

"Things like what?"

"Things like me talking to people."

"Jeeze," said Elaine, pulling a face. "Well, we gotta make camp. The sun will be setting soon, and we are no way near the town yet."

That's when I remembered that I was still at school.

"The sun? Oh darn. I gotta go."

"You don't turn into a wolf, do you?" asked Elaine, jokingly.

"No, I - never mind. I just have to leave."

I pulled out the book and read the first few lines. I didn't stop in The Library. I slammed down Elaine's book and grabbed for Alice.

When I landed, I was surrounded by darkness. The school was empty, and the cleaners were gone.

I was locked in.

CHAPTER 32

Iran to the main door of the school just in case, by some chance, it wasn't locked. I shook the door handle hard, but it was no use. If I couldn't get out of there soon, Mom would definitely freak out. We didn't live in a dangerous neighborhood or anything like that, but Mom was pretty protective of me, even when she was mad.

Especially when she was mad.

I tried to think of how else I could leave. There were the fire exits, of course, but they were alarmed, and I didn't exactly want to alert the world to my presence.

I rushed from door to door in the failing light, trying every one I could think of. They were all locked. Soon I was out of breath from running and collapsed against the wall of the corridor. My heart was beating hard in my chest. I tried to think.

There was a creak and then the sound of a door shutting. Footsteps echoed in the silent space. I froze, wide-eyed, trying to hear more.

It had to be a security guard. Who else would be wandering the school at night?

But now, what do I do? Do I make myself known to

them? Or do I hide and find another way out?

As quietly as I could, I opened the nearest classroom to me and snuck inside. I closed the door and gently let go of the handle.

The security guard's footsteps drew nearer. I couldn't help myself, I peered out through the classroom door to see if I could see them. The rhythmic swaying of torchlight flashed here and there. It seemed like they were just shining it on classroom doors.

I sighed in relief.

Within a few minutes, they had done their rounds, and their footsteps led away. Finally, I heard the sound of another door opening and closing, and I was alone once more.

"What are you doing here?" asked a voice in a loud whisper.

I screamed, and a shadow fell upon me, covering my mouth. I looked about wide-eyed, my heart racing like never before.

"Quiet!" said the voice. There was silence for a moment, and then the hand was withdrawn. "We are lucky he didn't come back."

"Who are you?" I said, trembling.

The light of a mobile phone came on and illuminated a face. It was Darcy. He raised his eyebrows in greeting.

"Darcy? What are you doing here?"

"You first."

"I just kind of got stuck here," I said, trying to find a credible reason. "I fell asleep."

"Bullshit."

"It's true! What are you doing here."

Darcy opened his mouth to speak but hesitated. "I sorta live here," he said.

"Live here? No, you don't," I said.

"I do. My home isn't safe."

"Oh," I said, wondering what that could mean. "Your parents?"

"Mom still thinks I live at home."

"And your dad? He doesn't hurt you, does he?"

"What? No. My father was a good man."

"Oh." By the distant look on his eyes, it didn't seem like it was a good idea to ask any further questions on that matter.

"Now tell me why you are really here," said Darcy, "I need to know."

"I told you, I just fell asleep. Now please, I need to get out of here. Is there any way out?"

Darcy shook his head. "Well, I get out through the window, but somehow I don't think that you will be trying that option."

"How come?"

"It's quite a drop."

"But I need to get out of here!" I said, panicking.

"I'm sorry, but unless you want to trip the alarm?"

"Well, I might just have to," I said. There was no way I could stay there. Any moment now, Mom would be calling me down for dinner. I would get in big trouble if she found me missing again without letting her know where I was.

"If you set it off, then I can't stay here tonight."

"And you definitely can't stay at your house?"

Darcy looked solemn. "I guess I could. Just this once."

I felt guilty, I didn't want him to get in trouble, whatever it might be. But there was no way I could stay the night at school.

Just then, there was the sound of a door slamming. The thud-thud of heavy boots running echoed through the school.

"Who is in there?" bellowed a voice.

Darcy and I exchanged glances.

"We are screwed," he said.

"There has got to be somewhere we can hide?"

He shook his head.

I looked at the book in my hand. Darcy followed my gaze. "What?" he asked.

"I think I know a place," I said.

CHAPTER 33

I snatched at Darcy's hand and opened Alice. He tried to pull away, but not in time. Soon we were tumbling into the book.

We landed right next to The Library's Heart. Darcy was sprawled out on the floor as if he had fallen from a great height. He wasted no time in getting to his feet.

"Where am I?" he demanded.

"This is The Library."

"Take me back now."

"It's OK, Darcy. I'm the Keeper here."

"I said, take me back!"

"But the security guard?"

"I have known many magical realms, Alex. None of them have been harmless. Take me back!"

He was kind of scary.

"OK, whatever. Fine. Take my hand."

By the time that we were back at school, it seemed the guard had moved on. Darcy looked serious.

"Where did you get that book?"

"It came to me. The Library chose me."

"What do you do in there?"

"I just look after the books, Darcy." I felt that now was not the time to go into detail.

"You freaked me out, that's all," said Darcy, clearly trying to calm himself.

"Understandable."

"Last time that happened, it was weeks before I got home."

"Last time?"

"Never mind. Last time was definitely not a library."

"OK," I said, my mind racing with questions.

"I guess this explains where you went during detention."

"Yeah. Sorry for lying about that."

Darcy's scowl broke into a smile, and he laughed. "It's not generally the sort of thing people share if they can help it."

I smiled. "I suppose not."

"Well, we still need to get out of here. Shall we risk the alarms?"

"I guess we are going to have to."

"Don't worry, I've done this heaps of times. When the door is open, we will need to run."

"I know."

Sirens blared as we fled, hearts pounding. The school was washed in white light. The school bell rang, shrill in the silent night.

We ducked into the bushes and out the other side. Within moments we were running down an empty suburban street. I was terrified, Darcy was laughing. After about a minute of running, I slowed to a stop. My lungs were burning, and I needed to cough.

"It's OK, take a rest," said Darcy, "we should probably walk from here, or it will look suspicious."

Darcy didn't appear to be at all fatigued from the sprint. "How are you not out of breath?" I managed to ask between gasps. He just shrugged.

"I run a lot," he said simply.

We walked through the streets. The smell of cooking dinners wafted through the air and mingled with the scent of suburban gardens. Street lamps washed the world in a soft yellow glow. We did not speak.

We got to Darcy's house first.

"I can walk you to your place if you like?" he asked.

"I'm sure I'll be fine."

He didn't look convinced.

"Your mom will probably be happy to see you," I said.

He gazed at his family home as if he were recalling a distant memory. "Yeah, she probably will be." He looked back at me and formed a troubled smile. "I miss her," he said.

"OK," I said, not really understanding all of his long silent pauses and meaningful looks. He reminded me of Batman, gazing down on the world of ordinary people and wondering what it must be like to live in such a pleasant place.

I was happy to be alone for the rest of the way home. Walking through the front door, I was flooded with light and the sights and smells of an evening with the family. Everyone seemed vaguely cheerful. I needed that. I acted vaguely cheerful too, and for one night, I tried not to think about Lilly and libraries and sorceresses.

The next morning, Lilly was waiting for me at the front gate. She greeted me with a soft "hi," and we walked into school together in silence. It seemed as though our conflict would just sorta be swept under the carpet, there to be tripped over another day.

Ordinarily, I would have been pleased to avoid the awkward conversation, but yesterday had really left me shaken. I didn't want to lose Lilly's friendship, not just to avoid the discomfort of making an awkward apology. Some awkwardness is worth it.

"I'm sorry," I said at lunch once we were seated around our octagonal table. "I really am."

"Forget about it," said Lilly, concentrating suspiciously hard on her sandwich.

"Please, tell me how I can make it up to you. It's not fair what I did. I just want to do the right thing."

"Don't worry about it. Just - next time, I just want you to think of me, you know? And how I'm feeling. With my insides. If we are friends, then we need to support each other."

"I promise I won't let you down again like that. Hey, why don't we set up another date?"

"Well, we can't go to the movies again, it was awkward as with just me and two boys."

"You still went?" Guilt flipped about inside me like an over-energetic rabbit.

"Yea."

"OK, not the movies then."

"What about the night market on Thursday?" she suggested.

I love the night market. Like, it's pretty much the coolest thing that there is in this part of town. It only comes once a month, and I often end up missing it because, well, you know, the humans and stuff.

"Sure," I said, trying to hide my hesitation.

"I know you, Alex. I know this is just the sort of thing to set you off. You know that you will actually have to speak to the boys, right?"

"Yes," I said carefully, "whoever they are."

"They are Daniel and Carl. Promise you won't flake?"

"I promise."

"Super," she said, with muted enthusiasm. I could tell that she was still quite upset with me, but at least this was a step in the right direction.

"You know how like people carve their names into trees while on dates?"

"Yeah, what about it?"

"Have you ever wondered why so many people carry knives on dates?"

"Weird, I guess," said Lilly.

***

I was on my way to class when Darcy appeared from behind a pillar. "Hey," he said.

"Hey."

"You want to put your library to good use?"

"What do you mean?"

"Some people could use your help. Badly. You think

you could spare an afternoon to save some lives?"

"Sounds reasonable," I said. Hank's jaw dropped, and he kicked my diaphragm.

"Is that a yes then?"

I met with Darcy at the front gate after school. I had never been driven by someone who was not an adult before. Hank did a few twists and turns in my belly as my seatbelt clicked into place.

"So, where are we going, anyway?"

"It's just a little way out of town." Darcy's eyes were on his mirrors, concentrating.

Silence.

It was awkward. I wanted to fill the silence with something, anything, but I had nothing I wanted to say.

Once we were on the highway, Darcy spoke. "What made you decide to help?" he asked.

"I'm not a toerag," I said.

"Well, you did hesitate. Maybe you are just half a toerag." He was silent for a moment. "Can we just pretend I didn't say that?"

"Sure."

Darcy started fiddling with the radio, but to no avail. "The tape player is stuck," he said, and I think something must be up with the receiver.

"That's fine."

"The tape in there is a Mozart compilation. I'll put that on?"

"Sure."

Loud and crackling, the grand voice of some German opera singer filled the car. I tried to listen to it, tried to focus on it, but with Darcy driving, my nerves, and the drama of a full orchestra, the whole experience was kind of terrifying.

"Can we turn it off?" I asked after mulling over it for far too long.

"You don't like Mozart?"

"No, I mean. I don't know. I just don't think I can deal with him at the moment."

"Fair enough," said Darcy. He switched the radio off, and we drove on in silence.

The view out the window changed from suburb to town and back to suburb again. Soon the houses were giving way to the occasional crop field and then finally wide open plains.

It was late afternoon when Darcy pulled over at a random point on the side of the road. I got out of the car and looked around. The country was hilly and smelled of cow manure.

"Where is this place?"

"Middle of nowhere, I would say. Kind of a good thing, actually. Come on, there is someone I want you to meet."

"You didn't say anything about meeting people."

"I said we are saving lives, right? Well, that involves people, you know."

He led me along a muddy path through a grassy field. It wasn't long before water started seeping into my socks. It was uncomfortable, but nothing compared to my apprehension.

We came to a low hill and started to climb. I couldn't see anything at the top of the hill and followed Darcy in silence. Occasionally we stopped, and Darcy looked around for the track. Once he spotted what he needed to spot, we changed our direction a little and continued on.

Eventually, we came to a crest. There, dark against the landscape, stood a girl.

CHAPTER 34

The girl looked to be about nine years old. Her clothes were caked in mud, and she had a very serious look on her face. Her hair was tied back in tight braids. She was standing next to a hole in the ground as if she were guarding it.

"Wes þu hal, Brunhilda," said Darcy to the girl. She nodded and then looked at me suspiciously.

"Alex, I would like you to meet Brunhilda."

"Hi there," I said. The girl looked at me with a puzzled expression and then looked at Darcy. "Does she speak English?"

"Yes, in a manner of speaking. But if you are asking if she can understand you, then the answer is no."

"OK, sure."

"There are five refugees trapped down that hole. Brunhilda here was able to get out. I found her wandering in the fields. She is small and could crawl through, but the rest of them down there are trapped."

"How did they get down there? Were they tunneling?"

"In a manner of speaking."

"Just tell me."

"Well, you know how I said that they were refugees?

Well, I may have given you a bit of a false impression. The thing is they are not just from another country, they are from the twelfth century."

"The past?"

"They are not the only ones, either. People have been popping up all over the place. Their village was remote in the north of England, but when the Normans invaded, it was inevitable that they would be discovered. When they were found, this particular tribe could expect to be destroyed, man, woman, and child. In their desperation, they turned to a wizard from the south. He offered them sanctuary, a way out of the foothills, and to safety. They had no place else to go. He created some sort of wormhole, and they all walked in. The wormhole must have been unstable because something went very wrong."

"Time travel?"

"Yeah. For us, this happened more than 800 years ago, but for Brunhilda, it all happened last week."

"This is crazy."

"And your magical library isn't?"

"How do you know all this?"

"Families of refugees have been turning up all over the place. It's been hard to talk to them as they speak an ancient dialect of English. These days we call it Old English, and only university professors and Tolkien enthusiasts ever learn any. I fall into the latter category. Most of them don't want to be found and are just trying to get by without being deported. The ones I did speak to helped me to understand what happened. Unfortunately, I still had no way of getting Brunhilda's family out."

I looked at the little girl. It broke my heart to see her standing guard over her family like this. Her expression did not change as we spoke.

"I did my best to get food and water to Brunhilda so that she could carry it down, but it wasn't until yesterday that I found a way to get them out."

"My library."

"Exactly. When you disappeared, I figured there was something different about you."

"Most people wouldn't have immediately thought of magic to explain a disappearing girl."

"Most people haven't see what I have seen," he said, smiling.

"So, what do I need to do?"

"I need you to crawl down the tunnel, find Brunhilda's family, transport them into your library, climb back out, and reverse the process. Can you do that?"

I froze. Hank squeezed all the air out of my lungs and then punched them.

"You will be OK," said Darcy, his tone steady.

"Sure," I squeaked.

Darcy said a few lines to Brunhilda in Old English. She looked puzzled but nodded and led the way to the tunnel. It smelled of clay and dampness. I crawled in after Brunhilda, holding my phone up to light the way. Soon I was covered in mud.

The recent rains must have flowed down here like a river. I imagined what it must have been like for the people trapped in a dark hole in the ground, a roaring storm in the world up above, water gathering at their feet.

The tunnel went much deeper than I expected. Brunhilda crawled fast, stopping now and then to make sure that I wasn't too far behind. She had a determination about her, which I had never seen in a child before. She formed an interesting contrast with Jonny, who was probably only a little younger than she was.

At length, we reached the end of the tunnel. I crawled out the end and then swung onto my feet. I cast my light over the cave. It was quite spacious, but more than half the space was taken up by a pool of muddy water. Figures were leaning up against the edges of the cave. They started to stir as they saw my light.

Brunhilda shouted something in her guttural dialect. A couple of the people stood up. She ran up to one that wasn't moving and kicked him hard. He groaned as she tugged on his arm until he was on his feet.

I just stood there watching, silent, not knowing exactly how this was going to pan out. Even while I was saving people's lives, I still worried about what they thought of me.

Soon Brunhilda had gathered her family into one spot. She then turned and looked at me expectantly. Nervous, I walked toward them and motioned for them to touch my shoulders. It felt awkward having the hands of strangers touching my arms and shoulders like that. One taller person had their hand on my head. I fumbled with the phone and the book, trying to get light on the page. As soon as I got the angle right, I started to read.

The travel to The Library was more intense than ever. This time among the swirling pages, half a dozen people were tumbling around me as well. I had just enough time to find the experience terrifying before we landed on the burgundy tiles of The Library.

My eyes were assaulted by the bright light of The Library's Heart. I looked about and saw the bodies of my companions sprawled around me. Brunhilda was straight to her feet. Now I could see just how bad a state these people were in.

I knelt down. "Make sure they don't wander," I said carefully. Brunhilda stared at me, blankly.

"Ic þæt ne undergiete," she said.

"No wandering," I tried, speaking slowly. Brunhilda squinted, nodded, and then looked back at the refugees, like a shepherd guarding her flock.

It didn't look like any of them were in a state to wreak havoc in The Library, so I turned to my book and returned to the cave. It was a longer journey back up than it was going down.

The dim light of the tunnel's mouth swayed before me. My arms were heavy with the effort of crawling. I was covered in mud, damp, and miserable. But that was OK because these people would be safe. I rested in the darkness for a moment, everything aching. Closing my eyes, I hardened my resolve and pulled myself onward.

CHAPTER 35

Everything go OK?" Darcy asked urgently.

The open air was cool and fresh, and the night sky was filled with stars.

I nodded and then opened my book to read.

When I got back to The Library, I found the refugees in the same formation as we had made when we left the cave. Brunhilda stood in front of them like a drill sergeant. It was almost unfair how much command she had over herself for so small a person.

We repeated the process, and soon five medieval refugees were out in the open air, dazed, but smiling. One rather tall woman gave me a bear hug. Her woolen tunic stunk, but as far as hugs go, it wasn't so bad.

Once released, I watched as Darcy unwrapped the cloth which bound his sword. He handed the sword to Brunhilda. Brunhilda shook her head and pressed the sword back to him. He nodded gravely, wrapped up the sword, and hid it away in his pack.

"Where will they go?" I asked Darcy as we watched the refugees celebrate their freedom.

"They will probably live in the hills for a while. The

world is a wilder place than people realize. There are lots of places where you can lie low if you need to."

Brunhilda, face as stony as ever, walked toward me, her eyes fixed on me. She stood there for a moment and then ran forward, wrapped her arms around my waist, and held me there in a feeling embrace. My heart swelled for her, and tears formed in my eyes.

The journey home was filled with a silence of a different kind. I was still wet and covered in mud when I got home. This time, I had remembered to text Mom to say I was going to be out but had no idea how I would explain the mud. At this rate, she would probably think I had secretly taken up a sport.

I shuddered at the thought.

Sleep took me quickly that night, and I slumbered deeply. When I awoke, there were a few moments when I felt completely at peace. It was a strange feeling.

Then I remembered about the date with Lilly and the boys tomorrow night. Hank took up a mallet and started thumping on my heart, which boomed like a bass drum. Ah, the old familiar beat.

It is all well and good saying that you are happy to go hang out with a pair of human males for an evening, but it is an entirely different thing actually going and actually talking to them.

All through Wednesday, I kept thinking about how it would go, imagining all the awkward things I would say, dreading the boy's expectations, fearing that I would look like I wasn't having fun, and worrying about letting Lilly down again. I did my best to try and avoid letting Lilly know how I was feeling, but I think she kind of guessed.

I wouldn't say that I overthink things generally. Most things I sort of block out or try to escape rather than overthink. Wednesday night, I was definitely overthinking.

Outfits are not exactly my thing. I had your standard assortment of jeans, long skirts, and embarrassingly revealing dresses that people who thought I should come out of my shell (Mom) always got me for Christmas, but I had no idea how you were supposed to arrange them into some sort of coherent look. No matter what I did, I seemed always to wind up looking quirky. That's not to say that I don't like quirky, but do other people like quirky? Is quirky OK?

After about an hour of pulling things on and yanking things off and generally turning my room into a home for lost garments, I gave up. I would just wear what I was going to wear to school anyway. It was the perfect solution: I would be comfortable, I could quit thinking about it, and I couldn't be accused of dressing up. I didn't want them to think I liked them, or that I didn't like them, I just wanted to get through.

I could just say I didn't have time to change between school and the market. Lying makes everything better.

I settled on a baggy maroon sweater and standard run of the mill black skinny jeans. Now I just had to decide on a bag. Was that a thing that mattered? I didn't know, but I didn't want to mess this up. I was going to be there for Lilly if it killed me, and judging by Hank's muted threats and occasional stabbing, death was definitely on the cards.

I grabbed the bag I usually carried Alice in and held it

up to myself in the mirror. It was then that I noticed that it was stuffed with flowers.

Frowning, I opened the bag up in full. Then I remembered. These were the flowers that I had picked with Elaine by the river bank. These were the flowers that she used to make tea...

Excitement seized me. After waiting until the family was asleep, I crept downstairs. The stairs creaked beneath my feet. Somewhere in the living room, some appliance was humming softly.

I set the kettle to boil and found my favorite mug. It had the face of young adult author John Green on it with the caption PIZZA. It's a long story.

Carefully I selected leaves and petals from the flowers and dumped them in the mug.

"Hi Alex," said a voice, I turned quickly, eyes wide.

It was Dad.

He rummaged in the fridge. "A little late for a cuppa," he said.

I moved in front of my mug, trying to block his view. The last thing I needed was for him to see that I was putting random flowers in a mug. He would probably think it was drugs.

Was it drugs? I didn't think so. Even so, I didn't want to process the questions. "Sometimes, you just need tea," I said.

"You sure do," he said, shutting the fridge and moving to the pantry, "and sometimes you just need crackers."

He rummaged around for a while longer, giving his snack selection what I considered an unreasonable amount of thought.

The kettle clicked off the boil, but Dad was still rummaging. I didn't want to pour the tea while he was still there, or he might see what was in the mug. Then again, standing there and doing nothing was equally suspicious. I leaned over to the kettle and switched it back to boil. It immediately switched off again.

Shoot.

"Right, night-night," said Dad, balancing a collection of crackers, cherry tomatoes, and hummus on one arm as he shut the pantry door with the other. Slowly, carefully, he left the kitchen.

All was silent. I grabbed the kettle and poured the steaming hot water into the mug. That same fragrant smell of licorice and cherries filled my experience.

I searched one of the kitchen cupboards for matches and a candle and then walked carefully up the stairs and into my room.

My heart was spinning with excitement as I shoved aside the clothes I had been agonizing over only a short time before.

Once I had space clear, I lit the candle and set it gently down on the carpet. It tipped a little, uneven on the uneven surface.

I sat with my legs crossed and brought the mug to my lips. I blew gently, sending steam swirling away in the candlelight. I took a sip. The tea seared my lips slightly. By the candlelight, I could see the dark shapes of the petals bobbing around.

I waited. The tea seemed to take an eternity to cool.

221

When at last I thought it might be drinkable, I lifted my mug and took a few choice sips. It was still too hot, really, but I couldn't wait any longer.

Setting the tea aside, I turned my attention to the candle. That's when I noticed something strange turn up in my mind. There was some resistance to trying the magic out, like, if I tried and it failed, then I would have lost something from this world.

I shook my head. I had to do this. Taking a breath, I pictured a rose.

CHAPTER 36

Nothing happened. The candle flickered and waved, but remained the same little light in the middle of a messy room.

I sighed with frustration and was about to give up when I noticed something. Tiny, almost imperceptible, a flower started to form in the flame. I blinked in disbelief, but it was still there. I smiled, focused on it, and willed it to grow.

Within a few seconds, the rose was blooming before me. It worked. It actually worked!

I did not dare to make it too large. I didn't want to start a fire. I marveled at this thing that I had brought into being by the force of my own imagination.

I marveled at the magic.

There was a thud from another room. I jumped, startled. Quickly, I blew out the candle and listened.

I sat in the darkness for a time. I considered lighting the candle again but didn't want to risk someone walking in.

This was my secret.

Reluctantly, I packed away the candle and climbed

into bed.

***

My stomach was all in knots the whole of Thursday. My mind spun from thoughts of the flaming rose to thoughts of embarrassing myself at the market. Never before had I experienced such a mix of excitement and dread.

And dread it was, but something was different about this dread. I knew in my heart of hearts that I had totally and completely resigned myself to going to the market that night. Such a feeling of resolve was a new experience for me, and I might have called it a good feeling, too, if I wasn't so uncomfortable.

Several times throughout the day, I caught Lilly looking at me wearily like I might betray some sign that I was going to leave her in the lurch again. It sucked, but there was nothing I could do. I just had to show up and prove myself.

The market took place in a car park underneath the mall near Lilly's house. When I got there, the roar of thousands of people bustling about the stalls filled the space. Food smells wafted through the air, some of them good, some of them not so good.

My whole nervous system was in revolt now. I wasn't running away like it said I should. At last, I was doing what was important. Hank was sulking.

I found a concrete pillar to lean against while I waited for Lilly.

It felt like everyone was looking at me. I tried to find

a position against the pillar that didn't look too awkward. There wasn't one.

After what seemed like forever, Lilly arrived. She was alone.

"You made it!" she said, smiling and going in for the hug.

"I said I would," I said, grinning stupidly at her, "where are the boys?"

"They aren't coming," she said.

"How come?" I asked, trying not to sound too relieved.

"I guess it's not about them. You love markets, and I didn't want to spoil it. I would much rather spend the evening with my best friend."

"You didn't think I would come, did you?" I said in mock accusation.

"Now, why ever would you go and say a thing like that?" she reeled off in a false southern drawl.

I could not have been happier. All I had hoped for was to get through the evening without being too much of a goof, but now I was ready to genuinely have a good time.

The market seemed filled with candles and flame. More than once, I wanted to see if I could make something in a flame, something small while Lilly wasn't looking. It was a delightful secret to have.

We bought two giant churros filled with warm dark chocolate and ate them as we wandered around. Neither of us were that keen on market food, but both had an extra stomach designated for churros.

We occupied ourselves rummaging through the stranger looking stalls. As ever, I spent a good deal of time looking at crystal and gem pendants without actually buying one. It was a well-established ritual. The simple ones bound up in netted string were the best, but I could never decide on one that was exactly right.

Laid out on several tables and shelves were crystals and fossils, old mugs and antiques, dried flowers and incense. An older man sat at some distance behind the table. His distance meant that I was free to browse without feeling watched.

One of the mugs, in particular, caught my eye. It was clay and crooked and utterly delightful. The mug looked like a far more appropriate vessel for brewing magical tea than my dearest Pizza-John. I picked it up and examined it closely while Lilly busied herself by looking at a trilobite fossil.

"What have you been drinking?" asked the old man quite suddenly.

I looked up, surprised, and almost dropped the mug. The stall keeper was no longer sitting back from the display. His face was only inches from my own. His gaze was steady like he was looking for some kind of truth in my eyes.

If he found it, then I would never know because just then, Lilly grabbed my arm and pulled me over to another stall where they sold anime figurines. I looked back over my shoulder, but the man was gone.

It was still relatively early when we finished at the market. We didn't get much of a haul, really. I lamented not purchasing the mug, but that guy had really creeped me out. I did, however, buy a tall lavender scented candle.

Because reasons.

We walked back to Lilly's house. Her mom and dad were lovely, but kind of glued to the TV, and I'm not talking about Netflix here. They had adverts and everything. I always forgot how annoying ads were until I visited her place.

Lilly's room was even more of a mess than mine. There were more shelves than could reasonably be accommodated in such a small space, and every shelf was packed with treasures. The whole room was a shrine to Lilly's eclectic personality. It had that distinctive smell that a place always gets when incense is burned there regularly.

She placed her new Goku figure next to the Vegeta she had on her shelf and admired the scene.

"Now they can be friends again," she said.

"Were they friends?"

"Sort of. Well, it's an expanded definition of friendship. Hey, we should light your candle."

"In this place? I'm fairly sure we would burn the whole place down."

"Nah, I burn candles all the time. Let's roll the dice, shall we?"

I laughed it off. "I should really head home."

"Alright. If you must."

"Thanks for, well, you know."

Lilly smiled, "I'm glad we talked things over, Padawan."

CHAPTER 37

Friday morning had that Saturday morning feeling. It had been a pretty exhausting week, and I was ready to leave school behind me and focus on the other infinitely more fascinating things happening in my life.

When, at last, I was free from the temple of doom, the sun was hot, and my mind was on Elaine and her quest. I didn't exactly want to fight any goblins or talk to any toll people, but I was ready for some fun, maybe even a little adventure.

Elaine met me on the outskirts of a small town just before sunset. The town was much smaller than the one in which I had first found Elaine and much more populated. It was defended by a high wall.

"What are we doing here?" I asked

"Come on, I know a place."

She led me through the gate and down a narrow street. I felt pretty conspicuous in my jeans and sweater. My canvas shoes were not exactly period dress either.

As we walked, I pondered whether it might be a good idea to start keeping some simple costumes somewhere in The Library so that I wouldn't stand out quite as bad.

I wondered how the Librarian would feel about that and pictured her standing over a heap of gathered clothing with massive fists at her waist, "what are *these* doing in *my* library?"

It wasn't long before we reached our destination. In appearances, it didn't look very different from the other buildings around it, though it was made of wood and not stone. The smell of deep-fried potatoes wafted in the evening air. The noises coming from inside were less enticing.

"A pub," I said, my tone level.

"Yeah, where else do you go to have fun?"

"Not to a pub."

"You are joking, right?"

She pulled me inside. The door swung dramatically as we walked in, a bit like a cowboy movie. The noise did not stop, though. These weren't the sort of people to pay attention to what was going on around them when there was drink to be drunk.

I think I read somewhere that if you spill a lot of your drink while drinking, then it wasn't called drinking anymore, it was called quaffing. If so, then these people were definitely quaffing.

I felt very uncomfortable.

"What will it be?" asked Elaine as she pulled out a barstool and sat down.

"I'm fine, thanks," I said. I looked around nervously at the very loud, very large, and often very ballistic patrons who swung, wobbled, yelled, and yes, quaffed, about the bar.

"I don't think so, book girl. I'm going to order you

something very large and very strong."

"No, really," I protested. I hadn't drunk before. Ever. I wasn't necessarily against drinking per se, but it just wasn't part of my life. This place was definitely not where I wanted to have my first drink. I always pictured my first time being at a restaurant with Mom and Dad, or maybe with Lilly watching some B-rated horror movie.

Elaine ignored my protest and gave the barman an order which I couldn't hear. I started to weigh up my options. I mean, I had come here just to chill out. I had imagined another bonfire or something with just Elaine, minus the animal cruelty if that was possible. Here I was well out of my comfort zone. There were so many people, so many loud, drunk, and scary people.

The barman poured out two drinks, and soon I was holding a mug full of an amber looking drink. It smelled faintly of roses and ginger.

"Have a sip?" said Elaine. She swigged a mouthful.

"Can't we go someplace else?"

"Nah. Hey look, those guys are playing Napkin."

"What's Napkin?"

"Man, please make sure that I never visit wherever you are from. I'm getting the feeling that it's not very fun there."

Elaine hopped off her stool and started nudging her way through the crowd. She dodged a man mid-topple by only a split second. Realizing this, she just laughed and kept on going.

I envied her. I wished I could just fit in like that. Not specifically with these people, but it would be nice to fit in with some group of people. Lilly was great and all, but

I guess sometimes I wish that I had more people around. Like a group or a place that didn't cause Hank to freak out.

I looked down at the liquid in my drink and wondered who it was at the bottom of the mug. Judging by my reflection, they were just like me, only a funny color, and slightly swirly.

I took a sip.

The drink tasted sharp and fragrant. I shuddered to think of how Elaine managed to drink as much as she had as quickly as she had. I tried another sip.

No, not today.

I put the mug on the bench and went after Elaine. It was like navigating a sea of sharks in there, except that there was no water, and the sharks were drunk.

At last, I found her inside a ring of people. They had gathered to watch her play Napkin against a man who was easily three times as massive as Elaine. Judging by what people were shouting, she was winning.

"Is that all you've got, friend?" she slurred, thudding her drink on the table.

"You amuse me, small person," said the man, "I have hardly started Napkinning to my full potential." He was clearly very drunk but was wonderfully articulate. "When I have done with Napkinning, you will be the floor."

"The floor?" asked Elaine.

"Under *all* the tables," he said flatly.

"Hey, Elaine!" I called, barely audible in a room full of noise.

"Alex! You're drunk!"

"That's you."

"Yes, it is. Well done, you drunk."

"Can we go?"

"And let this man tell everyone in the countryside, and the surrounding areas, that he is the Napkin King? And *I* am nothing but a handkerchief? A spare tissue? A wet wipe?"

"Wait, you have wet wipes here?"

"What's a wet wipe? Look, I'm not leaving. You can go if you want, but I finish what I start. Even if it means-" she looked at her opponent. He was collapsed amongst a mess of empty mugs.

"I win!" she said, jumping up and spilling her drink on her opponent, "drinks are on him!"

The gathered crowd celebrated by pouring their drinks on the man. Several started singing a celebratory song, but none of them sang the same song. This gave the general impression of audible chaos.

"Can this man get a napkin?" Elaine bellowed at the barman. There were cheers from everyone.

"OK, well, I'll just leave then-" I started, but paused mid-sentence as a drink was thrust under my nose. My eyes followed the drink to the hand that held it, up its owner's arm and to his face. It was Mason, grinning like a fool.

"Here you are, sa," he said.

"Oh, you shouldn't have," I said. I felt embarrassment course through me.

"Yeah, piss off," spat Elaine. She lifted her hands and started to weave her fingers.

The air began to crackle.

CHAPTER 38

Mason's hands erupted in flame. He dropped the mug that he was holding out to me and began to scream. He looked at me with mixed hurt and terror. The bar was silent now, but for his cries. He ran to the bar, and the bar man tossed a bucket of soapy water over his hands.

I looked back to Elaine. She was lying back on the table now, rolling in laughter, tears forming in her eyes. With one last look at the distraught Mason, I marched out of the pub and into the cold night air. It was way past time to leave.

The rest of my night was spent watching the fireplace in The Library. If the power that Elaine used to harm Mason was the same power I was learning to use, then I had to be more careful. Maybe I should stop completely? I certainly didn't want to turn out like Elaine. Apart from the concern that she clearly had for her sister, she seemed so unfeeling.

Would I end up like that?

The flames frolicked among the impossible logs of the fireplace. They were never spent, never needed replenishing, never destroyed by the sweeping flame. Mason wouldn't be so lucky. Right at that moment, he was probably in pain, cradling his hand, wondering desperately when they would heal up. I shuddered to think of it.

***

The next morning Mom asked me to hang out with Jonny while she ran a few errands. She was always worried that he would get lonely, but he was pretty self-sufficient. I sat with him for a while as he tapped away at some game on his tablet. It would take a lot to tear him away from that little screen.

"You alright there, Jonny?"

He nodded but kept his focus on the game.

"Are you winning?

"Nah."

"That's a shame."

"Why?"

"Um, most people like to win."

Jonny shrugged.

"Hey, I have an idea. How would you like to draw something with your big sister?"

"I'm not good at drawing."

"I'll teach you."

He dropped his tablet and looked at me with his deep eyes. "And then I'll be able to draw for real?" he said.

"Sure."

"That's amazing!" he jumped up from the couch and disappeared out of the living room.

"Where are you going?" I called.

"I got paper and pens in the cupboard," he said. "I got blue paper and yellow paper, and I'll bring it to you."

Before long, we were settled at the dinner table, felt tip pens sprawled everywhere. "So, what do you want to draw?"

Jonny stuck a pen in his mouth and looked at the ceiling, "um... Maybe a fairy?"

"A fairy? Are you sure? People shapes can be very tricky."

Jonny smiled. "You will teach me."

We sat together and scribbled and drew until Mom came home. When she was through the door, Jonny grabbed his fairy and ran towards her. It was a pretty good attempt for a first go.

"What's that you have there?" asked Mom when she had put down her bags.

"It's my fairy," said Jonny. "Alex showed me. I'm going to make it real."

Mom gave me an approving smile.

***

That night I was eager to have another experiment with candles and tea. I was nothing like Elaine, nothing like her at all. There was no way in a million years that I would deliberately hurt someone, let alone laugh about it afterward.

There were still plenty of flowers from my bag to make the tea with. As before, I waited until everyone was asleep before heading downstairs to boil the kettle. Once I returned with my tea, I sat with my new candle on the carpeted floor.

After a few strikes, my match lit, and I held it to the

candle. I hesitated, pulling my hand away. My room was still a mess, and would likely remain a mess for some time. I needed to find a place where I could practice this flame magic without risk of someone walking in on me, or accidentally burning the house down.

I blew out the match, drank my tea, and packed up my bag. I considered setting up in the backyard, but there were just too many houses looking down onto it with too many possible eyes on me. After a few moments of deliberation, I decided to go to the nearby park. There were a few clearings that were both private enough and open enough for me to sculpt with fire without any inadvertent vandalism.

The night air was cool and damp. I pulled my sweater tight around me. I wondered if my candle could make a flame large enough to keep me warm. I really had no idea what relationship the size of the original flame might have to the size of the things that I could create. Last time I only made a small rose in the candle flame, but that was for safety. I would not have to worry so much in the park.

It wasn't long before I found a suitable clearing. I knelt in the damp grass, steadying the candle on the ground. I had not thought to bring anything to sit on, so reluctantly, I removed my sweater and lay it on the grass. Goosebumps crept up my arm.

It was beautiful there alone with my candle under the stars. Even without the possibility of magic, I wondered why people didn't do this sort of thing more often. Of course, the stars were not as bright as the stars in Elaine's world. Light pollution washed most of them away.

There were not many sounds there in the park, just

crickets, and the occasional cry from some shy night bird.

I watched the candle's tongue of fire wave gently in a breeze for a moment and then began to focus. I knew what I would make first. I had been thinking about it all day. With my hands outstretched towards the flame, gently, I molded it, formed it, willed it.

The flame began to change.

Like before, it was gradual at first, but I was more confident now. First, her slender arms came into view, then slowly, there emerged the rest of her body. Her hair curled downward and waved in an imperceptible breeze. She turned about to face me and let her delicate wings unfold.

I wondered for a moment what Jonny would say if he saw that here in the park was a real fairy. I bid her dance about tiptoe on the candle. She flew, she twirled, she twisted. She danced amongst the flames beneath a starlit sky.

After a time, I sent her flying up into the night. Next, I formed a fawn, shy, and curious. It sniffed at me. It's soft eyes appraised me. I wanted to reach out and pet it but could tell from the heat that my fingers would burn.

"It's not safe out here," said of voice.

I swept the fawn away and turned to see Darcy standing in the shadows.

"Darcy?"

"I'm not even going to ask you what you are doing out here."

"I'm just-"

"I didn't ask."

"Right."

"I wanted to thank you for helping me the other day."

"It was nothing."

"For those people, it was everything."

I felt the heat rush into my cheeks. "How are they doing?"

"Fine, I think. Brunhilda was talking about you."

"Talking?" I tried to imagine her saying more than a few words together.

"Well, she asked if they had left any mud in your library."

"Oh, no. I don't think so."

"I'll pass that on."

"Thanks."

"Well, that's all I wanted to say."

"Thanks."

Darcy turned to leave. "Oh, one other thing."

"Yeah?"

"You shouldn't really be messing around with candle magic. That stuff can get you killed."

"It's not-"

"I know, not candle magic. Just try not to kill yourself."

With that, he turned and disappeared into the darkness. Once he was out of sight, I tried to settle back into what I was doing, but it was no good. I didn't know what Darcy had seen, and I didn't know if he was still out there. After a few moments, I packed up my things and went home.

***

Later that night, I lay in bed with wide eyes and a whirring mind. I wanted to sleep, but I could not get the fawn I created in the fire out of my head. The effect of its body cast in flame was unlike any art I had seen before. I was determined to share it with the world somehow. But how could I do that without revealing this new secret ability?

It was still early the next morning when I started working on the drawing. I was determined to get this phantom out of my mind and into the world. Soon I was in a trance of lines and curves and textures. Time absorbed me. I was lost in my art, forming what I had formed in flames, trying to capture its essence, its movement, its vitality.

When I finally finished my creation, it was well past lunchtime. The fawn gazed out at me with curious eyes, waiting for me to pet it.

I transferred the image to my phone and opened up Instagram. Lilly had provided me with the password to the account that she created. She had also gone to the trouble of following a bunch of people, including my dad. Awkwardness was just around the corner.

I only had the vaguest idea of how Instagram actually worked. I knew it had hashtags or something, but I wouldn't worry about that. I just wanted it up there, there to be seen.

Soon it was all done. I had finally put a drawing on Instagram. I felt nervous and excited. It made me smile to think that the first picture would not be a dragon. I gazed at my gallery of one with pride.

CHAPTER 39

With my drawing done, I lay back in my bed and let my mind wander. It was probably time to take Lilly to The Library. She was my best friend, and If I were to continue spending hours and hours inside of The Library's collected works, then I would probably need at least one person in my life who understood where I was.

Something had changed within me since I found the book, it was hard to put a finger on what, but I needed to share that something with Lilly. I grabbed my phone and sent her a brief message:

GoT?

Soon she was walking in through the front door.

"Hi, Mrs. Alex's Mom," she said as she took off her shoes, "I'm here to train your introvert."

"With television, I hear," said Mom.

"Gradual exposure is the most effective method of de-sensitization," said Lilly.

"I'm sure it is," said Mom.

Once we were in my room, Lilly went about the usual process of setting up the TV. I watched her, wondering if our lives would ever be the same in just a few moments.

"Hey Lilly, I want to show you something."

"Give me a second."

"Don't worry about the TV. This is more important."

"More important than watching Game of Thrones for the fifth time?" asked Lilly, spinning around and covering her mouth in shock.

"Yeah," I must have looked serious because Lilly's eyebrows dropped into a frown.

"What's up?" she asked, compassion hanging in her looks.

"Oh, nothing bad. It's this." I held out Alice.

"An old book! Cool," said Lilly, grabbing for it.

I pulled it away from her, noticing that I was shaking as I did.

"An old book that I'm forbidden to touch?"

"Kinda. Look, this book isn't an ordinary book. It's kind of a portal."

"That's what my dad always used to say about books when he was trying to get me to read more. Are you trying to get me to read more, Alex? Are you my dad?"

I smiled. How do you break it to someone that the normal world is not normal at all? I guess you just gotta show them.

"Take my hand," I said.

"O...K...," said Lilly, hesitantly closing her fingers around mine.

I opened the book and began to read the first line.

"Alice was beginning to get very tired," I said aloud.

"Oh, storytime!" said Lilly. Well, that's what she was probably going to say. What actually came out was more along the lines of: "Oh, story ti-aahhhshoot."

Together, we plunged and plummeted through the whirling pages and the airless air. I felt awful for how scared Lilly must have felt at that moment, remembering my first encounter with The Library. But there really was no other way.

Within moments we had transported from the quiet of my suburban bedroom to the largest library that ever there was.

I was pretty used to the procedure by this point and generally landed on my feet when I came through. Lilly, on the other hand, lay sprawled, face down on the tiles.

"You OK?" I asked, cocking my head.

Lilly rolled onto her back and stared up into the endless ceiling.

"Gnorts," she said, "what happened to your roof?"

"This is my other house," I said.

Lilly sat up, leaning on her elbows, and looked around. "Am I in a library?"

"Yup."

"Why am I in a library?"

"Well, you know how I said portal. Well-"

"You meant a literal honest to god portal. Like a wormhole in a book?"

"I guess so," I said, imagining a worm burrowing through my book and wondering how I would go about re-homing such a worm.

"Alex! There is so much room for activities!"

"An interesting reaction."

"This is a freaking library, Alex! You have been keeping this in your bag? It's kind of like your own little Tardis. No, this is way cooler."

"Please keep your voices down in The Library," said the Librarian, peering down at Lilly with curiosity. "I wish you would tell me before you bring friends here, Miss Reed."

"Sorry," I said.

"By the way, have you seen Mr. O'Connor? I seem to have lost him."

I shook my head.

The Librarian shrugged and returned to her work.

Lilly watched as the Librarian started climbing up one of the shelf ladders. "Is that a gorilla?" she asked in a whisper.

"Yeah."

"Does she know?"

I stared at Lilly blankly.

"Well, show me around, would you? I wanna see all the things."

"This place is too enormous to see all the things. But I can show you the pretty cool things I have found so far."

I led Lilly to my reading nook, and she met the black cat. It trotted up to her and rubbed its face on her leg.

"You have a kitty!"

"Well, I don't think it is mine. I think it belongs to itself."

"You are so progressive, Alex," she picked up the cat and wrapped her arms around it, "I'll be coming back to visit this kitty. You know that, right?"

"Of course," I said, smiling.

We sat down, and I started wondering about how I would tell her about the stories. She seemed to be handling

The Library fairly well, but Elaine's story was another thing entirely.

"This place is so cool," said Lilly, almost to herself. "It's so you, Alex, you know that? It's like Alex Heaven. Wait, you're not dead, are you?"

"I hope not. If I am, then at least there are books."

I led her through rows and rows of shelves, wanting her to see everything through my eyes. She ran up to a book, picked it up, and started flicking through. I hurried to her side and managed to close it before she read anything.

"You have to be careful. Don't read the books, OK?"

"But it is a library, Alex. What else do we do here?"

"We can read them later, but just wait for me to pick one, OK?"

"Yes, Dad."

I placed the book back, and we continued through The Library. Soon the familiar blue glow of the Library's Heart was casting its soft luminescence over the shelves around us.

"This is very strange," said Lilly, "where is this light coming from?"

I stopped Lilly a few meters away from the hovering orb. "This is The Library's Heart."

"Is the library depressed?"

"Just don't."

"Because it's blue."

"I know."

"It's depressed because it's blue."

I nodded. "I see the connection."

"Blue."

"This is a piece of the void of creation," I said. The words sounded weird in my own voice, "It's where the books draw energy. It's where all creation draws energy. It is outside of time, and it is outside of space."

"Can I touch it?"

"No. The Librarian was very clear on that. If anything goes in, then something has to come out apparently, and that is a really bad thing."

"You say that, but now I just want to jump in. Thanks, Alex."

"You are a worry. OK, next spot on the tour is the maps area."

"It's going to have to be pretty amazing to top the spinning lightning orb of creation. Next time lead with the maps and build up to the orb."

When we got to the maps area, Lilly immediately started running from one to the next. She shook her head and then ran to another map. "What are you doing?"

"I'm trying to find my house, of course. Wasn't that the first thing you did?"

"Honestly didn't occur to me."

"I don't even know these places. Oh cool, a map of Middle Earth!"

"Really?" I said, running over. I looked through the glass at the map. It was the same as was printed in the front of Tolkien's books. Unless I had missed something, then this map would lead me straight to his world. Did that mean it was real?

I could spend some serious time in the Shire, but that would be for another day. Lilly wandered over to the next map and then the next. I was in the midst of looking for a map of Hogwarts when I heard Lilly scream.

I darted to where she was standing, but I was too slow.

Lilly was gone.

Chapter 40

Aglass cabinet was open, and there on the floor was a map of someplace called Pai. I picked it up and tried to figure out where Lilly might have been looking. After scanning the map for a moment, I saw that there was a place labeled The Witching Well. That had to be it. I pressed my forefinger to the map and fell in.

I found myself sitting in a cafe. It was warm here, too warm for the sweater I was wearing. I scanned the area, looking for anything out of the ordinary. There were a lot of people walking about. They looked like travelers.

Lilly was sitting at one of the tables, apparently scrolling on her phone. She looked up and saw me.

"Alex, oh my god, we are in Thailand!" She held up her phone for me to see the map she had pulled up. A couple at the next table gave us a look.

"Here you are," said a woman, placing a coffee in front of Lilly.

"Thanks," said Lilly, picking it up and taking a sip. "What?" she asked when she caught my look.

"You ordered a coffee?"

"It's a coffee shop, Alex. Hey, you wouldn't be able to

tell me how to get back to The Library once you have gone through a map, would you?"

"You just press the map," I said, looking at the map in my hand.

"I didn't get a map," said Lilly looking around.

"I think maybe I'm the only one who gets maps."

"Oh, Miss Ladeedah. Well, I'm the only one who gets coffee," she took a sip, "it's good too."

It was nice there, just too warm for me. Once Lilly was done and had paid the lady with the wrong amount of money in the wrong currency, we returned to The Library.

"So that was cool. You are right. I mean, a piece of the void of creation looks good on paper, but instant travel without airfares? The maps definitely win."

"There is one other thing that I want to show you."

"Don't tell me its better than the maps. It's not possible. I'm all about the maps."

"It's possible."

I led her back to my nook. Picking up Elaine's book from the shelf, I sat down and opened it up.

"Reading time again?" asked Lilly, her look skeptical.

"Well, you know how we can go into the maps."

"Yes."

"Well..."

"Miss Reed, are you telling me we can go in?"

"That is indeed what I'm telling you."

"Huh," she said distantly.

"What?"

That's when I noticed that she was holding a book. I cocked my head to read its title. It was Darcy's book. "We can't go in that one," I said, snatching it from her.

"Hey, why not?"

"Because it's rude, Lilly. It's like his diary, only a lot more personal."

"An excellent reason to have a look around."

"No."

"Come on! He is so mysterious."

"He has reasons for being mysterious," I said. I immediately regretted betraying that I knew more about him.

"You read it didn't you?" asked Lilly. She grabbed hold of the book and ran across the room.

I stood up, my heart pounding. "Give it here!" I said. It was like I was talking to a dog.

Lilly smiled, her eyes twinkling. She opened the book and began to read.

"Lilly, no!" I rushed forward but was not in time. She was being sucked into the pages of the book.

Almost as soon as the book hit the ground, I had picked it up again and was reading the first line.

Dad was away on one of his trips...

Once I had landed, I found that I was standing in the hallway of a house. I guessed it must have been Darcy's family home. Up ahead, Lilly was standing in a doorway, one hand on the frame.

Quietly, I walked up behind her. Her eyes were fixed on something in the living room. I peered over her shoulder. There, curled up on a couch, was a boy. His face was red and covered in tears. He was sobbing to himself and clutching an orange sweater. He held it tightly to his chest. He held it and wept.

It was Darcy, but Darcy as I remembered him from middle school.

I tapped Lilly on the shoulder. She turned to me, her eyes now filled with tears as well. She nodded and wiped the tears from her cheeks. "Sorry," she mouthed and tried to smile.

Turning away from the scene, we returned to The Library. We sat quietly for a moment, processing what we had seen, wondering what happened to that little boy, wondering what happened to Darcy.

"What do you think that was about?" Lilly asked.

"I don't know. Do you remember if anything major happened to him? I mean, people talk."

"No, nothing. I guess whatever it was, he kept it to himself. Do you think there is some way we could find out?"

"I think that if Darcy wants to tell us about it, then he will tell us about it."

"Yeah, I guess you are right." Lilly sighed and smiled at me weakly, "so what's this book you wanted to show me?"

We landed on the shores of a stony lake. I looked about for Elaine, but it seemed like this was one of those times where the book dropped me a little way off from her.

Then I saw Mason. He was down by the lakeside, apparently bathing his hands. I felt a pang of guilt. Though I knew logically that what Elaine did to him at the bar wasn't my fault, it still felt like it was my fault.

"Hello there," I said, walking cautiously towards him. My feet crunched in the large pebbles. It was a nice day there, but cold.

"You know this man?" asked Lilly, putting on a voice.

"Kind of. I have run into him a few times."

He didn't notice that we were there until we were almost right behind him. He looked up, eyes wide.

"Hello-" I started.

"Stay away from me, sa. I mean, miss. Just you stay back!"

"I'm sorry about what happened the other night."

"What did you do?" asked Lilly. She was clearly finding it all very amusing and didn't seem to notice the distress I was in.

"Wickedness, that's what. My poor hands," said Mason, holding them up in front of his face and inspecting them, "I can hardly eat, let alone carry me gear. The flourishing has taken a turn for the worse too. I'm a damaged man!"

"Let me see if I can help you," I said. I was not used to having such pain and anger directed toward me. I felt very uncomfortable.

Mason stumbled back, put his hands back to ease his fall, and then howled in pain when he landed on them.

"Look what you've done now!" he screamed.

"I'm sorry-"

"Just go!" he said.

CHAPTER 41

I wanted to cry. Lilly was now looking suitably worried for the man. "Come on," I said, my heart full.

"His hands," she said.

When we were well away from the lake, I found a tree to fall against. I wanted to find Elaine and tell her to go fix what she had done. I didn't even know if she could heal Mason's hands again. The way he looked at me really shook me. It was like he thought that I was some kind of monster. I looked vaguely at my hands. Was I a monster? I remembered the way Darcy looked when he found that he had been transported to The Library.

"What happened to him?" asked Lilly, kneeling down next to me and placing a hand on my shoulder.

"It was the other night. Elaine set his hands on fire. I don't know why, but she did."

"Well, she sounds like a piece of work," said Lilly.

"She's just had a different sort of life, alright?"

"I'll bet," said Lilly, "but it doesn't mean it's your fault, OK? She is an individual and makes choices of her own. I mean, I could say something about you choosing to spend time with her, but I won't."

"This is her book, Lilly. I kind of have to help her out. It's my job now."

"Most people who get part-time jobs at the library just file books away and mind the desk. I mean, there are definitely perks to this place, but just remember that you can't save everyone. You can walk with people for a while and help them on their path, but what they do is up to them. And sometimes what they do is set fire to people's hands. Any librarian who expects you to fix that in your spare time is asking way too much."

"I guess."

"Now, it's been a pretty freaking incredible afternoon, Alex. I mean, I challenge you to top it, like, ever. You have definitely become my favorite for the next Doctor. But right now, I think maybe it's time we go back to the real world and watch some Netflix."

I smiled. "Sounds like the best."

***

The following evening, I decided it was time to confront Elaine over what happened on Friday night. I mean, she was drunk, but that's no excuse for setting a man's hands on fire. And it is not really an explanation as to why she laughed so much about it.

I knew what Hank wanted. Hank wanted to avoid the subject and pretend that nothing happened. But I was starting to realize that Hank pretty much always had the worst plans, and yet I always put him in the driver's seat. It sucked, but I was going to have to confront her.

I found her in the wilderness, pulling herself through some thick grass. I waited for her ahead in the path. She must have noticed my expression.

"What's up?" she asked.

"We need to talk."

"About what?"

"The man whose hands you set on fire the other night."

"You don't happen to know where he is, do you? I wonder if he has a firm handshake. He did such a good job screaming. He deserves a high-five." Elaine scanned my face with wide and laughing eyes, waiting for me to join in.

"He was really hurt, Elaine."

"He will heal."

"Elaine, what you did to him sucked. Like, seriously sucked."

"What I did to him was freaking hilarious. What is it with you, Alex? Do you know him?"

"His name is Mason. He is a good guy."

"What do you want me to say? I'm sorry OK. I find this kind of thing hard."

"What kind of thing would that be?"

"This whole 'what you're supposed to do around other people' thing. When Tabatha was around, she helped me with that. She helped me with what was right and what was wrong. Without her, I have lost my compass."

"Well, yes, I can see that it sucks, but you have got to stop hurting people." I thought of the fox for a moment. "And hurting animals for that matter."

"Oh yeah, you were so funny about the fox."

"OK, that wasn't funny. And can you just not do that

kind of thing again?"

"Geez, Alex. Well, I guess I'll try. You always come up with the worst kinds of games."

I breathed a sigh of relief. The confrontation was over.

We walked through the scruff and brush. As we walked, I noticed the beauty of the place. Where at first it seemed to be a land of dead and dying plants, I started to see the little things. There were the little white flowers which clung to old rocks, the rabbits here and there scurrying out of our path, the circling eagle overhead searching for its prey. It was unlike any land I had been to before. It was open and windswept and dramatic. I wondered what it would look like when it rained.

We had been walking for perhaps a half-hour when we came to a stream. It was not a wide stream, but it was not one that we could pass by hopping from rock to rock.

I took off my shoes and socks and held them in one hand. With the other arm waving for balance, we crossed the stream. The water was crisp, cold, and quick moving. I wondered if the water had come directly from those mountain caps, thawing in the spring sun and rushing over the plains.

Once on the other side, I pulled my dry socks over my wet feet. It felt strangely comforting. I had just pulled on my shoes when Elaine froze.

"What is it-" I started, but she raised her hand to silence me, scanning the horizon.

"Come with me," she said in a whisper.

She crouched and started edging down a side path. I did likewise, bending low. It didn't take long for my legs to feel like they were going to fall off. When Elaine stopped again, I fell to a knee. We were at the top of a small hill, and there was a clear view of the surrounding area.

"They are near."

"Who are?"

"Goblins. Look!" Elaine pointed to someone standing in a clearing. It was Mason. He was talking loudly and pulling on something, something big.

"Pickles!" cried Elaine.

Sure enough, a giant harnessed duck was being dragged reluctantly out into the open.

"We have to help him."

"No we don't, he has my duck."

"Elaine, that's the man who you set on fire."

"Well, he is doing very well for himself. Increasing in assets."

There was movement in the grass. At first, all I could see was motion, but then I saw them. Some two dozen figures were snaking towards Mason, leaving behind them a trail of dented grass.

"They will have him soon!" I said urgently.

"Lucky us, I guess. They will take him back to camp now, and we will have a night of not having to worry about goblins. Sounds like a win-win."

"That's not a win-win at all."

"Isn't it? Well, it still works out for me, so that's OK."

I couldn't watch him get caught. "Come on, Hank," I said, getting to my feet, "let's do some good." I scampered down the side of the hill.

"Who the F is Hank?" asked Elaine.

CHAPTER 42

I needed to make some kind of distraction so that Mason could get away. But what? My sudden movement had caused a few of the goblins to look back over in our direction, but as of yet, none had started my way. From this distance, they looked like nothing more than stooped figures. Elaine joined my side.

"What do you think you are doing? We will just get caught alongside the duck thief. Be smart, let's go."

"We need to create a diversion. Any ideas?"

"We could sneak off as quietly as possible. That would be fun."

"Come on."

"Look, Alex. Being caught by those things is no party. What do you think they will do? Put us in a nice little cage with a view and ask us about our opinions on important matters? No, they will poke you full of holes just for the pleasure of watching you writhe as you bleed to death in the dirt."

"That was graphic."

"No, really?"

"So you are just going to let that guy get killed like that?

He probably wouldn't even be in this mess if it weren't for you."

"Stop it with the guilt trip already."

"You haven't shown even the slightest hint of guilt!"

"Look, fine. If I help him escape, will you shut up about his hands?"

"I think that's a fair trade."

"OK, let me think," she covered her mouth and frowned. "Wait, do you hear water down here?"

"I think there is a creek."

"Good, we can use that." She darted off into the thick shrubs. I followed after her.

"This isn't a trick, is it?" I called as I ran. I almost collided with her as she looked out over a shallow stream, gurgling its way down from the mountains.

"There isn't much power here," she said, shaking her head. "Come on, we will need to make sure that we are as close as possible to the goblins."

There was a shriek.

Elaine and I made eye contact and then hurried along the creek, tracing it closer and closer to where we had seen Mason. At last, we got to a curve in the creek where it bent away from the scene. It was as close as we were going to get.

"What are you going to do?"

"There are spirits in every stream," said Elaine. "They linger in natural bodies of water. These are where the barriers between worlds are at their thinnest. Streams like this one are close to a very particular sort of afterlife."

"Afterlife?"

Elaine looked at me, eyes sparkling. "The dead," she

said.

"Right. The dead. This is fine," I said, trying to keep my head level.

Elaine brought her hands together as if in prayer, looked up, and then separated them. A thin band of white light formed between her palms. She manipulated the beam in an intricate weave of movement.

The creek gushed and swelled.

I watched, wondering what I was about to see tumbling down those rocks. Surely there was something less creepy we could do to distract the goblins?

There was a sound from somewhere in the shallows of the creek. A neighing?

Then, quite suddenly, a shape cantered out of the water. It was a horse made entirely of still flowing water. It tossed its head, reveling in its freedom.

The horse might have been an impressive sight if it wasn't for the fact that it was only a foot tall.

Another horse appeared and then another. Elaine directed them toward the goblins, fierce concentration fixed on her face.

Soon there were dozens and dozens of the horses galloping through the undergrowth, leaving a spray of fresh mountain water wherever they went.

They were pretty freaking adorable.

After a time, Elaine's arms began to wilt, and she dropped them, collapsing back. I caught her in time, and she steadied herself against me.

"They are pathetic," she said, watching the last of them disappear.

"They are amazing."

"These are the spirits of the great horses of old. They deserve better than a creek."

"They deserve a cuddle."

Elaine shook her head. "Come on," she said, leading me off after the horses.

We could hear the goblins before we could see them. There was a shriek, then another. "Get em," one bellowed.

We entered the clearing just in time to see the panicked clan hacking at something at their feet. It was quite comical. Mason had seized the opportunity to mount the duck and was now trying to control the beast, which was itself quite spooked by the horses. It took off on its own accord, fleeing for its life.

The goblins were shorter than people and had sickly green skin. They were draped in furs and armor that looked like it had been scavenged. Their faces were almost entirely made up of solid nose. Their eyes were tiny and black, and their ears were long and full of rings.

Elaine was laughing.

"We did it," I said, smiling.

"Yeah, I guess we did. Not quite as powerful as if I had a great river, but I have to admit that it was effective."

"Can you teach me how to do that?"

Elaine smirked. "You want to learn how to summon the dead? Somehow I don't think it's quite your thing. No offense."

I was prevented from replying by a sudden voice.

"What have we 'ere," it said.

Startled, we spun around.

CHAPTER 43

Elaine and I were back-to-back now. There must've been around thirty goblins all waving their spears at us, cursing us, asking frequent questions.

"Which of you is the human?" asked one.

"Come on, Grek. You can't just ask which one is the human," said his companion.

"Where are your weapons?" asked another.

"We don't have any," said Elaine.

"That's embarrassing," said one of the goblins.

"Would you like to borrow one?" asked another goblin.

A spear cracked against his head. It sounded like it must've hurt, but he didn't so much as flinch.

"You can't just go around lending humans weapons, you fool. It fosters dependence. I mean, there are just two of them now, but just you wait. Will you be willing to hand out weapons to the hundreds of humans that will come to this land when they hear about your free weapon give away?"

"They just look so sad."

"You know what? We should take them back to the village. That will cheer them up. Have a nice roast. Bit of a singsong."

"We are fine, actually," said Elaine, "we may look sad, but that's just because humans have upside-down faces. Well known fact."

"Do you want me to turn yours up the other way?" asked one goblin, menacingly.

"No."

"This one is tricksy. Time to tie 'em up," said the goblin with the most impressive looking hat. He was apparently their captain.

"Let's have 'em for dinner."

"We could cut off their legs and feed them to each other. It ain't so bad if you eat someone else's legs. Doesn't count."

I inched my hand towards the bag containing Elaine's book.

"Don't move," said Elaine in a whisper, "those spears are poisoned. If they manage to catch us with one of those, then we won't be waking up tomorrow."

"That's a nice thought," I said. Dread drenched me like sudden rain.

"Now, are we going to have to tie you up, or are you going to play nicely?" asked the captain.

"We'll come, we'll come," said Elaine.

"I don't like that quiet one," said the one called Grek. He pointed a knobbly finger my way. "Can you say something, please? She is creeping me out." His voice was higher pitched than his companions, and he was short, even for them.

"Everything creeps you out," said his more threatening

friend.

"Humans, especially," said Grek.

"Hello," I said. The goblins looked at me, confused. Shoot, even goblins think I'm awkward.

The goblins led us single file down a long and winding trail. It vaguely followed the river for a time and then veered off towards the mountains, joining up again with the river further east. The foothills of the mountain range were densely wooded. The sun was setting now, and the first of the evening stars twinkled in the sky.

After my initial shock at seeing these creatures, I relaxed a little. They continued to threaten us periodically, but these threats were punctuated with such innocent banter that it was hard to take them seriously. They even walked comically, waddling this way and that, bumping into things, scratching themselves at every opportunity. I also had the comfort of knowing that it would only take me a moment to disappear. They could not point the spears at us forever.

Underneath the tree's canopy, small lights were lit. It gave the impression of a music festival. A very budget music festival. I had never been to a music festival, but I had seen pictures. The goblins themselves lived in a great variety of makeshift huts and hovels. Some had fires inside, the smoke rising up through the center, weaving through the trees and into the night. Others were cooking in the streets, roasting small objects on tiny spits.

I got the feeling that they did not see outsiders very often. There was not a single pair of eyes in all the village that did not look up to see us as we walked.

"What have you got there?" was the most common phrase uttered as we walked. It wasn't said so much with curiosity, but with all the insinuation of an old drunk trying to remember what it was like to have a good time.

Now that they were home, the goblins lost discipline and scattered. Soon there was only a handful guarding us, despite the best efforts of their captain. The remaining goblins lead us through the village and out the other side, then down a muddy path and toward another river.

The river was wide and weedy. They maneuvered us onto a rickety raft and rowed us over the inky dark waters to a small island. The island might have formed from years of gathered silt and a few enterprising seedlings. In the center, the goblins had erected a cage of iron.

They shoved us into the cage, and a great lock was put on the door.

"You can't eat iron, can you?" asked Grek.

"They are humans, not elves," said the captain.

"So, they can eat iron?"

The captain looked uncertain. Another goblin whispered something in one of his ears. "Not very well," he said. "Anyway, little humans, have we got something in store for you?"

"How would they know?" asked Grek.

"We have Gormfull in store for them," said the captain.

The goblins started laughing together and climbed onto the raft.

"Just you wait!" called out one of the goblins as they rowed away.

"It is not as though we can do anything else," muttered

Elaine.

"What do you think Gormfull is?" I asked.

"It is probably some chicken they call a shaman, or a goddess made of sticks. I don't know. Goblins are messed up."

"So, how do we get out of here?"

"It seems like we have been in this situation before."

"Yeah, but I was on the other side of the bars last time."

"And a lot of good it did you."

"I freaked out okay, I'm sorry."

"I know. I'm only kidding," said Elaine.

"Can you do anything with the water? Like, make a horse?"

Elaine looked at me with incredulity. "Oh yeah, summon the spirits of the dead twice in the same day. That sounds like a fantastic idea."

"So, that's a no?"

"Hey, why don't you do the disappearing thing you do."

"What about you?"

"Come back for me, of course. You just need to reappear on the other side of those bars and then get the key to let me out. I think the one by the tree there has it. He has to fall asleep eventually, right?"

Sure enough, a shadowy figure was now getting himself comfortable by the base of a great tree.

"I can do that," I said.

CHAPTER 44

Wait, it looks like they are coming back," said Elaine.

I peered across the water. A goblin with a particularly large head was climbing onto the raft. He rowed toward us. A strange permanent smile wended across his green face. It was not a pleasant smile. It was the smile of someone who did not know what else to do with his lips.

Once he was on shore, he waddled up to the cage and introduced himself.

"Pleasant evening, ladies. My name is Gormfull. They call me Gormfull because of all my Gorm," he tapped his head. "Got it?"

"You keep it in your head?" asked Elaine.

"Bang on."

"Takes up a lot of space, does it?"

Gormfull looked puzzled for a moment and then launched into his speech. "I have been sent to speak to you as a sort of ambassador for the Goblin Nation. We are a small nation, a small nation of small beings, but we are a proud nation. However, we have never been recognized as a legitimately established government amongst the peoples. It is my 'umble request that on this suspicious day, we start the all-important talks towards goblin recognition."

"I think that wherever a goblin goes, he will be recognized," said Elaine.

"That is very kind of you to say, madam. However, it has been the experience of myself and my brethren that Goblin Kind are not recognized wherever we go. We are treated as a nuisance, as pests, as murdering outlaws."

"Well, you are, aren't you?"

"Look, miss, murdering isn't outlawed for us goblins. Semantics, see?"

I wasn't sure if I had anything to offer this conversation. But it struck me that there might be some good social justice that could be done here. I couldn't exactly rely on Elaine to draw that out, so I gave it a go.

"Gormfull, hi, speaking on behalf of humans, I was wondering if it were possible for goblins, that is to say, the Goblin Nation, to consider some reforms in their laws around murder."

"Oh, please," said Elaine, audibly rolling her eyes.

"Speaking on behalf of myself," said Gormfull, "I would be perfectly willing to have a look at that. I have hardly murdered anyone at all. It's just not really in my nature. Never really acquired the taste. Gave it a go, sure. Life is short. But I'm afraid that I never quite understood it."

"Great," said Elaine.

"But unfortunately for you, and myself, I do not make the rules around here. Goblins are very particular about leadership, you see. I don't quite fit the mold."

"How do goblins choose their leaders?" I asked.

"By election, generally. Oh, and threats. The threats are a vital part of the process."

"I thought there was something about a sword and a lake," said Elaine.

"Yeah, we gave it a go for a while. But we had to give that up. You see, too many of our good goblins got lost in the lake."

"They drowned?"

"No, it was a very confusing lake. Good goblins would set out, and they would wander about for days and days. Some would starve out there. There was even another community started on the far side of the lake."

"They couldn't make it back?" I asked.

"I'm afraid not. I lost a cousin that way."

"Why couldn't they just build a raft? Goblins build rafts," said Elaine.

"Well, you would think that might work. But it was so much fun firing arrows at them as they frantically paddled their way back over. It was tragic. Fun-tragic."

"Look, if we promise to speak to the rulers of the human lands, will you just let us go?" I asked.

"What about letters?"

"What are you talking about?" asked Elaine.

"Humans, they are always sending these letters. We figured out that they carry little packets of magic with them. We got stacks of them. Won't say how we got them," he tapped his nose, "some of us burn them along with the socks on special occasions."

"So, what do you want us to do with them?"

"I want you to make some."

"You want us to write letters?"

"Yeah. Lots of 'em. Letters can change the world."

"OK... We are going to need quill and paper," said Elaine.

"What's that, then?"

"Like a stick to make marks with and a very large white leaf."

"White leaf, huh? I would never have guessed. Let me see what I can do. Don't go anywhere," he said, chuckling.

The strange creature clambered back into his raft and rowed ashore.

"What an interesting person," I said once he was out of earshot.

"That's very kind of you to call him a person. Now let's make a move before he gets back."

"What do I need to do?"

"I have been watching the guards, the ones on patrol, they seem to be coming by every five minutes or so. We will need to time this just right. I don't imagine they look over here very often, but just in case, we will wait till they have made a pass and then you can make your move. When you are back here, swim ashore, get the key, then come let me out. We need to do all that before the guards get back or before Gormfull returns. Can you do that?"

I was fairly sure it would not be a problem except for swimming in the water. It was dark, and it struck me that it was quite dangerous to swim in unknown waters at night. But I couldn't exactly leave Elaine in this cage.

"All right, I'll do it."

"Wait until I give you the signal. Once they are gone,

you have about five minutes. Please don't leave me here. I don't think I could take another conversation with that Gormfull guy."

"He was all right."

"Yeah, but the politics! It's not what you expect in jail. Why couldn't he hit us with rocks or something?"

"I thought it was interesting."

Elaine gave me a look. Then she glanced to the shore. "Go!"

I opened Elaine's book and read the first line. Hardly had I landed in The Library before the book was snatched from my grip. I gasped, reaching for it.

"What is that you are reading?" screeched a voice.

CHAPTER 45

Elderly Elaine towered over me. She was holding her own book now, peering at it suspiciously. My heart pounded in my chest. Now that I knew who she was, I was able to trace Elaine's likeness. Time and bitterness had not been her friend.

"I can't read the title. That is strange, strange indeed."

"Please, I need it back."

"Patience, young one. Why such a rush? It's only a book. You read it, I read it, it remains the same."

"Sometimes."

"Ah, so it *is* that kind of book. Why don't I have a read?"

"No!" time was ticking. The goblins would be back at any moment. If they realized that I wasn't in the cage, then who knows what they would do to Elaine. I thought of those poisoned spears. I thought of Elaine bleeding out in the dust.

The old woman opened the book to read. I held my breath.

"This book is empty," she said with a scowl.

"I know," I said, "I am going to write a story."

"Waste of time," barked Elaine. She threw the book at me. It collided with my nose and pain shot through my experience.

"Hey, that hurt!" I called after her as she walked away.

"I don't care," she said.

Fortunately, the book was not blank to me. As soon as the woman was out of sight, I began to read.

I found myself on the outside of the cage as we had planned.

"What took you so long?" asked Elaine immediately on my return.

"My book was, well, never mind. Guess I'll be swimming then."

"Yes. Please."

I placed one foot into the dark waters. It was far colder than it looked. Reluctantly, I started to wade into the shallows. I couldn't tell how deep it was going to get and hadn't thought about the book. I didn't want to get it soaked. Who knows if it would still work. Every extra step forward brought the water higher and higher up my waist.

"Hurry up!" hissed Elaine, "you don't have much time!"

The 'encouragement' really didn't help. Frantically, I scanned the river bank for any sign of the guards. It had to have been almost five minutes by now.

At its deepest point, the water reached my chest. I held the book overhead to keep it from the river's grasp.

There was no time for celebration once I was on the shore. The guard with the key was leaning against a thick tree trunk next to a large candle. I crept towards him as silently as I could.

He didn't look like he was a very heavy sleeper.

Two oversized keys hung on a tree branch next to him. All I needed to do was grab them and go.

My heart was beating fast as I approached. It was hard to believe that the guard couldn't hear it thudding around in my chest.

I was inches from the keys when he stirred. I froze, watching him roll over. He placed one green hand over the branch that kept the keys.

I didn't know what to do. If I tried to lift his hand now, I would surely wake him.

A noise caught my attention. The guards were returning. They were arguing loudly with each other. It was unclear exactly what it was about, but the subject seemed to be eggs.

I was out of time.

Then an idea struck me. It had been a while since I had drunk of the flower tea, but it was possible that there was still some power left in me. I directed my attention towards the candle, pouring all my concentration toward it, focusing with all my might.

The flame began to grow.

Slowly, carefully, I breathed life into the flame. I didn't want to hurt the guy. It's not exactly his fault that he was a goblin. But I could make him uncomfortable. Very uncomfortable.

All I needed was one: toss or turn, and it didn't matter which.

I could see sweat beading on his forehead. It was working!

I took a moment to glance up. The guards were in sight.

Now or never. I had to grab the keys, whether it woke him or not.

I reached out my hand. It was shaking in the candlelight. I was just about to snatch the keys when the goblin turned over. I grabbed them.

As quickly as I could, I hurried toward the water's edge.

"Oi!" yelled one of the patrolling guards, "what are you doing out of your cage? Get back in there!"

"Ingratitude!" called the other guard as the water reached my waist.

The shouting must have woken the sleeping guard because there was commotion by the tree. I glanced back briefly to see that the two goblins had abandoned their pursuit of me to go watch a fire that had started at the base of the tree. The candle must have been knocked over in the confusion.

A smile broadened across my face. I couldn't help it. I'm such a badass.

That's when I felt a slither against my lower leg. My smile dropped, and I cried out involuntarily.

"What is it?" asked Elaine urgently, "you didn't drop them, did you?"

"There is something in here!" I quickened my pace.

"Oh yeah, didn't tell you about the eels. I should probably have told you about the eels."

"Eels? Was that just an eel? It was enormous!"

"Aren't eels big where you are from?"

I tried to remember if I had ever seen an eel, but could

only picture the vacant face of one gormless creature I had seen in a book.

"Don't worry, they are usually well-fed around here. Goblins aren't great swimmers."

I clambered onto the shore, my clothes dripping, thankful to be out of the water. I chose one of the keys at random, shoved it into the rusty oversized lock, and gave it a twist. The lock popped open and dropped to the ground.

Elaine stepped out of the cage, dusted herself off, and peered into the water.

"What are you doing?"

"Trying to figure out if there is another way across. I don't really want to get my feet wet."

"You couldn't have done that earlier?"

Elaine shrugged. "Well, it doesn't look like there is. Good thinking with the candle, by the way. Though, if it were me, I would have just started by setting fire to the tree. And the goblin."

Glancing over to the shore, I saw that the tree was now completely aflame, bright in the dark night. About a dozen goblins had gathered around to look at it.

"Do you think we can get past them?" I asked.

"They seem distracted. Goblins are pretty weird about fire. Hey, you can go back to your world now if you want. I'm probably OK from here. And maybe, well, maybe I can handle the Hollow Hills on my own, you know? You have already helped me out. I don't want to put you in any more danger. Tonight was a close one."

The nearer we got to the Hollow Hills, the more I wanted Elaine to say something like this. The sorceress sounded pretty terrifying. But the more I got to know Elaine, the more I was convinced that I was supposed to help her. If I didn't, then who would?

"What? No. I said I would help you, and I will."

"I'm serious. You should probably stay away from me anyway. I'm not like you, you know."

"We don't have to be alike to be friends."

Elaine gave me a long hard stare. "Alright, OK. Your funeral. Thanks though, I don't think I have really had a friend before."

"Just your sister?"

"What? Yeah, that's right. My sister. That's why I gotta save her. Now get back to your world, would you? There is no sense us both getting soaked."

CHAPTER 46

On Tuesday evening, Lilly insisted on accompanying me back to The Library. I couldn't blame her, the place was epic, but I was apprehensive of her meeting Elaine.

I took Elaine's book from the shelf and opened it to the first chapter. The book was always nearby when I wanted it, just as the Librarian said. Taking up Lilly's hand, I began to read, and we began to fall.

Night had spread over the land. The stars were bright in the sky, but little of their light penetrated the forest canopy to light our way. Elaine was somewhere else. I looked about for Mason, but couldn't see him anywhere either.

"It's so real," whispered Lilly.

"It is real," I said.

"Yeah. Hey, so this is a book about night time?"

"No, this is a book about that girl I told you about. Elaine. She is like an actual person, though, not just a character from a story. It's a little complicated."

My eyes were adjusting to the night now. There was life in the shadows. Small glowing insects glided gently through the air on their mysterious errands. The woods were alive with night sounds. An owl hooted loudly and deliberately from somewhere just behind us.

"So what do we do now?" asked Lilly.

"Whatever we like. I don't know. I usually just walk in a random direction until I run into Elaine."

"She hangs out in a random direction, does she?"

"Apparently. Look, be careful around her, OK? She is kind of a handful."

There wasn't really a path to follow. Disturbed fireflies flew up as we walked. They hovered and spiraled about us, casting a blue-green glow over the ferns and undergrowth.

As we walked, the forest closed in around us. It reminded me of the living woods in The Lord of the Rings. It seemed like the trees were alive and wanted to hold us. Maybe they did? Eventually, we reached an impasse and stopped.

"This place is nice and all," said Lilly, "but I'm not really in the mood for dark fantasy at the moment, especially the one about slightly annoying scratches from bumping into things. Not my vibe."

"It's usually not like this," I said. Usually, I ran into Elaine way before this. Was it possible she was staying away because of Lilly?

"Why don't we just try another book? Maybe one set inside? On comfy couches, maybe?"

"This story called me, I think. I sorta have to see it through."

"Well, you ain't seeing anything at the moment."

"There is this sorceress I gotta help Elaine deal with," I explained.

"Oh, yeap."

"She sort of eats people."

"I vote new book."

"We are not far from the Hollow Hills now," said a voice. It was coming from above. There, in a tree above us, crouched the shadow of Elaine.

"Gnorts, that's dramatic."

"Gnorts?" asked Elaine.

"Don't ask," I said, "if you ask, then she wins."

"So, you have brought a friend into my world."

I nodded, feeling awkward.

"I'm Lilly," said Lilly, holding out her hand to Elaine in the treetops.

Elaine looked at it. "Charmed. I'm Elaine," she then turned to me, "will she be accompanying us tonight?"

"Yeah, I guess so," I glanced at Lilly.

"I'm all about the quest life," said Lilly, "just show me the way."

Elaine jumped down. "We will arrive at the Hollow Hills within the hour," she said.

"What do we do when we get there?" I asked.

"Leave it to me," said Elaine, "just stay close, OK?"

I nodded.

Elaine shot Lilly a strange look and then led us into the night. It turned out there was a path we could have been walking along. It was like an actual cobbled path, and it was pretty much right next to us.

"I'm getting serious off-vibes from her," whispered Lilly when she got the chance.

"She's alright really," I said, "just a little rough around

the edges. Like you."

"You are mistaking me with the post-apocalyptic ba-dass version of me. Don't worry, I understand, we look very similar. But seriously, just keep your book handy, so we can get out if we need to."

I lifted up the book for her to see. My index finger was inside the pages, marking the space we needed to open to.

CHAPTER 47

Elaine led us out into an open field. Blue grass stretched before us like a ghostly sea. Hundreds of standing stones stood in the field. They seemed to be set in an elaborate pattern.

"Come on," said Elaine, gleefully.

"She seems cheerful," said Lilly, giving me a sideways look. "I don't like it."

"You would be cheerful, too, if you were about to rescue your sister from the clutches of an evil sorceress."

"It seems to me that Elaine is an evil sorceress, just saying."

"I wouldn't say evil..."

"You told me Sauron wasn't evil, Alex. Freaking Sauron."

"I just said that if you look at his history that-"

"Yeah, I know, Alex. Everyone is really good and nice on the inside."

"I think that there is some good in everyone."

Lilly shook her head. "I love you."

I squinted at her mockingly and smiled.

Elaine was quite far ahead of us now. We quickened

our pace to catch up. The blue grass rippled and swayed in the silent wind. There was no sound in the field but for our legs brushing the grass.

Soon the stones were all around us, dark shadows in the night. Elaine was in the center of the circle now and appeared to be sitting on something.

"I don't see any hills, Alex," said Lilly, eyeing the stones suspiciously. She gasped.

"What is it?"

"Gnorts, that scared the carp out of me. I thought they were just stones."

I looked closely at the nearest shadow. The shadow changed from a standing stone to a statue.

"They are people," I said.

"Giant serious people," said Lilly. "Look, Alex, I'm really not feeling comfortable about all this. Can we please go back?"

"They are just statues. I'm sure Elaine will explain when we reach her."

"It's not the statues that worry me," said Lilly.

Once we passed the figures, I could see that there was a raised stone area in the center. Elaine sat on a stone chair in the center of that. She stood up on the chair as we approached.

"We finally made it, Alex," she said.

"What is this place?" I asked.

Elaine smiled. She thrust her hands into the air and shouted, "Claudere Caelum!"

Lilly and I exchanged urgent looks. My hand darted down toward my bag, toward our escape.

A great white dome of light crackled into existence overhead, covering the clearing, trapping us in. I didn't want to wait to see what this meant. We needed to get out of there. The book was open, chapter one was open. I read.

Nothing happened.

"Come on, Alex!" yelled Lilly.

"I'm trying!"

I repeated the first line and waited for that feeling of falling, but it didn't come. Panic was rising in my heart. I tried reading the next sentence.

"It's not working!"

"Run," said Lilly and started for the woods.

CHAPTER 48

I followed after Lilly as best I could. She was faster than me but looked over her shoulder now and then to ensure that I was still behind her.

That's when I saw the shadow close in on her. "Lilly!" I shouted. But it was too late. One of the statues had intercepted her path and wrapped two stony arms around her.

She cried out.

I tried to get to her but tripped and fell hard on my side. As quickly as I could, I was on my feet again, but now the shadows were closing in around me too.

Hundreds of faceless men.

There was nothing I could do. They had me.

They led us back to Elaine, who was again sitting on the stone chair, one leg crossed over the other. It looked like a throne.

Something had happened to her clothes. No longer did she wear the tattered travel garments which I had grown used to seeing her in. Her dress was all folds and lace, black as the night. There was a small birdcage next to her within which was a parrot, half-starved, and weak. She smiled smugly.

"I win," she said.

"Elaine, what is this?"

"This is me winning. Did I stutter?"

"Your sister?"

"Suits being a bird, doesn't she. Far less of a know-it-all. Hey, maybe I should turn you into a bird too?"

"You are the sorceress? You are Vicious?" I couldn't believe it. I mean, I knew that we had quite different views on things, but this?

"Told you so," said Lilly. Her voice was thin and weak, and she was dangling where she was held by the statue.

"Do you like my friends?" asked Elaine, following my gaze. "Well, they were my friends once. I had them killed."

"Killed."

"Yes, and then I bound their immortal souls to these golems so that they can do my bidding for all time. Much more efficient than friends. Didn't you wonder why they looked so sad?"

Their empty eye sockets were hollow and devoid of emotion.

"Now give my friend there the book, would you?"

"What book?"

"I'm not an idiot. I can't see it, but I know it is there somewhere. Hand it over."

"I'm not giving it to you."

"Alex, come on. We are friends. You don't want this silly thing anyway, do you? All the responsibility of being a Keeper. It is so much of a burden."

My blood ran cold. "How do you know about that?"

"My sister," she said, striking the parrot's cage. "This

bird. She didn't know how to use what she had either. She wasted hours and hours going on silly little adventures in meaningless books, never once questioning what she could really do with the power of The Library. The power of the Library's Heart and the void of creation is infinite. Oh yes, I know about those things, Alex. I have seen them. Every night when I close my eyes, I see them again. Limitless power, and now within my grasp. Give over the book, Alex. You can come with me. There is power in you, I can sense it. You would make a fine apprentice."

"I'm not giving you the book."

Elaine looked pained by my refusal but seemed like she was trying to hide it.

She nodded to one of the golems, and it wrenched the book from my hands. She surveyed the scene, seemingly checking all of the golems in turn. Two larger golems approached her, one carrying the book. They leaned toward each other, palms pressed against the book, creating a sort of an archway.

I struggled against my captor's grip. Lilly wasn't moving now. They must have hurt her pretty badly. I winced as I remembered how Lilly had warned me about Elaine. How could I have been so stupid?

Elaine began chanting in a low monotone. "Apertum est magnum bibliothecam."

"What are you doing?"

Her voice grew louder now. "Apertum est magnum bibliothecam. Apertum est magnum bibliothecam!"

The plain filled with a warm red light. It seemed to be coming from the golems themselves. The light flowed as if on a breeze toward Elaine, who then channeled it toward the statue-archway.

Was she trying to get into The Library? What have I done?!

Elaine's chanting grew to a crescendo and then suddenly stopped. She walked up to the archway, her dress trailing behind her. "Open," she said.

Light erupted from the archway, bright and white.

My heart sank. There before me was The Library, clear as anything. Elaine's face was joy, pure and simple.

"Come on, Alex, let's see what lies within."

I was carried forward, through the portal, and into The Library. Soon, light was all around me. We were in the center of The Library. The Library's Heart spun slowly and majestically on its invisible axis.

Lilly was carried in after me. The rest of the golems followed. They moved into a formation around The Library's Heart. Another spell?

"Here is all the power that there is, Alex. That's what Tabatha couldn't understand. All the power that there is, raw creation itself. It's about time a piece of that creation was in mortal hands, don't you think?"

"What are you going to do?"

"Simply make an exchange. You see, whatever goes in must be displaced. We will make a small sacrifice, Alex, and I will make sure I am in a position to receive what comes out."

The golem carrying Lilly started to walk towards The Library's Heart.

"Sacrifice?" my voice was quavering.

"I was going to sacrifice you, but I actually quite like you. This one, on the other hand," she gestured towards Lilly, who was just starting to stir, "the multiverse can probably do without her."

"You can't!" I said, tears welling up. I couldn't think straight. How could this be happening? I should be at home in my bed right now. I should be drinking hot cocoa and reading. It shouldn't have come to this.

"You sound just like my sister. Maybe I'll throw her in there as well."

The parrot squawked, but without much enthusiasm.

"I'm going to let you watch, Alex. I think it will be good for you. It won't take long. My friends are almost all in position now."

The golems had formed a circle, knocking down some shelves to do so. I wondered where the Librarian could possibly be. How would she feel about all this wreckage?

Four golems then lifted Elaine up and held her above them so that she was close to the Heart's equator, almost touching.

She nodded her head.

The golem holding Lilly carried her towards the Heart. She was fully awake now and struggling.

"Lilly!" I shouted, but it was no use. "Lilly, I'm sorry!"

I watched helplessly as my only true friend was marched toward her certain death.

CHAPTER 49

"What do you think you are doing?" bellowed the Librarian. She was standing on an upper floor, her great fists against her hips.

She jumped.

Elaine arched her neck upward just in time to see a 600-pound gorilla hurtling towards her. She tried to dodge, but not soon enough. The Librarian crashed into the golems, sending them skidding across the floor. They carved deep grooves into the tiles.

"I always knew that you were bad news," she said, towering over Elaine.

"No! I am so close!" Elaine screeched.

The golem dropped me and thudded forward towards the Librarian. The rest of the golems broke formation and did likewise.

The Librarian was strong, but surely she couldn't fend off that many giant stone creatures. They were soon piling on top of her. Every so often, one would fly into the air with a great thrust of a giant hairy arm and land some distance away.

I wanted to help, but what could I do? Lilly was still

being held tight. I ran towards her but was intercepted by three golems. I backed away. They stepped towards me.

There was a rumbling quack.

"My lady!" called a familiar voice. I spun around just in time to see Mason emerge from the portal seated on the back of Pickles, his sword flourishing. He charged forward, colliding with the golems in front of me.

"No way!" I heard Lilly say, staring at the giant duck.

Everything was chaos. The Librarian broke away from the center of the action and joined the duck, back to tail feather.

"Good to see you again, Mason," said the Librarian.

"Just in time, sa. Where is Lady Tabatha?"

"She's in the cage!" I yelled.

Mason looked at me. He seemed uncertain but nodded.

The circle of golems closed in around them, blocking them from view. Elaine was with Lilly now. She grabbed at her, and Lilly struggled in vain.

It was going to happen, and there was nothing I could do to stop it.

Hank was destroying my insides now. I had never been so afraid. I sunk to the floor. There was only so much more of this I could take. I glanced about for Alice. The book would be nearby now that we were back in The Library.

I grabbed it from a nearby shelf.

By rights, I should be safely in bed. With this book, I could be in bed. It would be so easy just to open up the book and read, open up the book, and escape back to my own life, warm and comfortable. I could let this be the horrible nightmare that it was. I flicked to the first chapter.

Hank was just too powerful.

Anger coursed through me. I threw the book to the ground. It skidded away under a shelf. Hank had made decisions for me for the last time. I took a deep breath and got to my feet.

"Do your worst, Hank. I'll do my best."

I stood tall.

My left hand swung downward, palm forward, and fingers outstretched. I felt the fire kindle. I took a step forward. My right hand swung down likewise, and a second fire erupted from my palm. I took another step forward, then another. My face contorted with anger. Anger at Elaine, anger at Hank, anger at myself.

I held my hands out front, wrists together, fingers spread. The flames collided and ignited. They burst forward like a flamethrower but with the force of a fire hydrant.

I drew what I pretty much always drew. I liked to start with the eyes, making them fierce, capturing that cold and ancient intelligence. I then used that start to guide the position of its jaw and the shape of its head. Its torso and its legs started to emerge, now a tail. It was the final touch that always gave me the biggest thrill: its wings, unfurled and unafraid.

CHAPTER 50

The dragon arched its neck upwards and silently roared. It flew up, then weaved and spiraled about The Library, flying high above the Library's Heart, surveying the scene. I guided her downward, twisting, and curling towards the battlefield. She collided with the first of the golems with a splash of sparks and flame.

She then blasted through another and another, leaving behind it a trail of charred remains.

A few of the golems tried to strike the flaming beast, but there was nothing they could do against a creature that lacked a solid form.

"Careful around the books!" bellowed the Librarian, "we don't want a fire like the last one. I'm still upset about that."

I threw the dragon towards Elaine.

The golem holding Lilly dropped her and jumped in the dragon's path, shielding Elaine from the full force of the blast.

Lilly didn't waste any time and scampered towards me, falling over her own feet in her haste.

I settled the dragon to rest on an upper level, surveying

the scene. None of the golems were left standing now, all were a crumpled ruin.

Elaine was scowling at me. She was still some distance away, but I could see that tears were running down her face. "I really thought I had found a friend in you," she said. It seemed like she was trying to hold back the full intensity of the emotion she was feeling. "I really thought I could finally find peace," she shook her head.

"Go home, Vicious," said the Librarian, compassion in her tone. She adjusted her spectacles.

Elaine shot the Librarian a look. She shook her head and smiled. "I have a far better idea."

The Librarian's eyes widened with sudden realization. "No!" she said, bounding forward. But she was too slow.

Elaine waved me a final goodbye and jumped into the void of creation.

"No!" bellowed the Librarian again.

The Library's Heart started to pulse. Its spherical shape was destabilizing. A fork of lightning struck a nearby shelf. Then another, then another.

The Librarian turned suddenly about. "Get away!" she yelled.

I grabbed Lilly's hand and pulled her back behind the nearest bookshelf. The dragon vanished out of existence.

"Back further!" the Librarian said as she passed us. Mason waddled Pickles briskly on. He was holding the bird's cage in one hand and the reins with the other. His wooden sword was tucked under an arm.

Lilly and I hurried after them. Another fork of lightning struck the place where we had just been standing.

At a safe distance, the Librarian stopped to catch her breath. We watched as the storm rolled over the shelves leaving a trail of destruction in its path.

CHAPTER 51

What does this mean?" I asked, placing a slightly singed hand on one of the Librarian's enormous arms.

"You remember how I said that some books held a taint?"

"Like Darcy's?"

"Yes, like your friend's book. Well, this is worse, much much worse. That lightning is the raw energy of the void. Every book it is touching will be changed."

"Changed? How?"

"Magic isn't a common thing, Alex. Only a relative few books have ever come in contact with the void and survived. My heart aches for the worlds within those pages."

"I could do with a little magic myself," said Lilly, nursing a shoulder, "I hope it strikes my book."

"Maybe it has," said the Librarian.

"Cool," said Lilly, raising her eyebrows.

"No, girl. That would be a terrible thing. Magic can be wonderful, but it can also cause immense suffering. If I were you, I would hope my book is well away from this storm."

"Will the storm pass?" I asked.

"In time, yes. And then we will have our work cut out for ourselves."

I gasped and fell to the floor. It felt like I was struck in the stomach, suddenly winded. The pain was immense. I cried out.

"What's wrong?" asked Lilly, crouching by my side.

"I think it's the call," I said, clutching my abdomen.

"You poor girl," said the Librarian.

"Why? What does the call do?" asked Lilly.

"Right now, Alex is feeling the call of hundreds of books, all at once. She will have to read them all. The task is enormous. You will need to be strong, Keeper."

CHAPTER 52

"Alex! Dinner is on the table!"

"Just a minute, Mom."

I pressed dial, and the phone began to ring. It was picked up.

"Hi Uncle Jack, its Alex... Yeah, Mom did say something about that. I'm just calling to let you know that I will be busy over the summer. A lot of reading to do. What? Yeah, for school... I know, it sounded like a good deal. Yup, OK. Yup, I'll let her know you said hi. Thanks, Uncle. Bye."

I was just about to go down to dinner when I saw that Jonny was standing in the doorway of my room. He gave me a funny smile and nodded.

I frowned.

"What are you doing there?"

"Nothing," he said, and ran off downstairs.

***

"You don't have to go just yet, Mason. I kind of like having you around," said the Librarian.

We were in The Library, and Mason was standing in

front of the portal back to his world. We were not able to shut the portal down, so the Librarian moved the two golems down to a basement level where it could be locked safely away. The room was dark but for the light of our torches and the daylight from the land beyond the shimmering arch.

The Librarian had provided Mason with new motley, and he was looking a lot better for having had a week resting within the most magnificent library that ever there was.

Mason held a cage containing Lady Tabatha, the most recently retired Keeper of The Library. She was looking much healthier these days but was, unfortunately, still a parrot. In his other hand, he led Pickles by a silver harness.

"Sorry, sa, but I must. The Kingdom of Avonheim needs its ruler."

"Will you be able to turn her back?" I asked.

"No idea, but we must try."

Pickles quacked.

"Well, if you need anything, just come on through. This room will be locked, of course, but I'll be down here from time to time."

"That is very kind of you, sa."

"Your hands are all better?" I asked.

"As good as ever they was, sa. I am sorry for, er, blaming you, sa. Had I known you were the Keeper-"

"-then we might have avoided a great many things," finished the Librarian.

Mason smiled and gave an awkward bow. "Farewell!" he said and disappeared through the portal.

The Librarian and I took our time walking back up

to the main level. With Mason gone, it was time to focus on the work. "That was quite an impressive spell you cast, Alex. I only wish that it weren't a fire spell. The books can be very sensitive to fire."

"Sensitive?"

"Perhaps flammable is a better word."

"But what I don't understand is how I was able to do it without the tea. Elaine said that the tea helped to tilt my mind, or something."

"That sounds right. Maybe your mind is just a bit angular nowadays?"

"Maybe, but I can't seem to do anything in the flames anymore."

"Probably a good thing."

"Yeah," I said, though I disagreed fiercely.

We emerged into The Library's main level. The Librarian had done a fairly good job tidying it up, but still, there were streaks of ash marking where the battle had taken place.

Something caught my attention: a golem. "There is one still here!" I said, walking over towards it. The Librarian followed.

"Quite inert, I think you will find. I thought about moving it, but I can't see any harm in leaving him where he is. Looks quite stately, if you ask me."

"It looks terrifying."

The Librarian sighed. "Well, I can move it if you like. I just thought Mr. O'Connor might want to have a look at it."

"Oh, did you find him then?"

"No, I'm afraid not," said the Librarian thoughtfully.

"It's OK, you can keep it here," I said, "you are the one that lives here, after all."

"But you will be spending a lot of time here, Alex. Now the storm has passed, it is time that you started addressing your duty."

My stomach lurched. "There are just so many of them," I said.

"You don't have to do it alone, you know. Have Lilly join you, or that Darcy fellow."

"Darcy? But is it safe?"

The Librarian shrugged. "Comparatively," she said. "I can help out a little too, though my place is in The Library. I can start having a flick through the affected books, do some reading ahead."

"You can do that?"

"One of the special privileges of being a Librarian," she said. She adjusted her spectacles and grinned.

***

The next day, I met Lilly for lunch at the usual spot. So much had changed, and yet so much had stayed the same. "Y'all got any lamps?" she asked as I sat down.

"Could you quit it with that already?"

Lilly laughed. "So, how did it go?"

"I did it."

"Gnorts, Alex, that's incredible!" she gave me a big ol' bear hug.

"It's just a speech," I said, my face smushed.

She pulled away and gave me a satirical look. A smile burst over my face. I felt so fantastic that I wanted to cry.

"So what does gnorts mean, anyway?" I asked.

"You are kidding?" asked Lilly, her face dropping.

"What? No."

"All this time."

"Yeah, why? What does it mean?"

"It's short for Gnorts, Mr. Alien."

"Oh, I see."

Lilly sighed and laughed. "Thank goodness for that!" she said, "you really had me going for a moment."

It was a good day.

"So, with the speech out of the way, I guess this means that you and Hank are friends now?" asked Lilly.

"Friends? No. I don't think we are friends. Not yet."

"So, how did you manage the speech?"

"Hank and I have come to an arrangement."

"An arrangement?"

"Yeah. He's allowed to do what he likes, but on one condition."

"What's that?" asked Lilly.

"So am I."

The End

313

I hope you have enjoyed your time with Alex and Hank.

Please consider leaving a review on amazon.com or goodreads.com. Indie authors eat or starve based on reviews they receive and I am extremely thankful for every single one that I get.

Available Now! The second book in the series, *Call of Kuyr*, is available for purchase from amazon.com

Sign up for my mailing list at jcgilbert.com to receive a free ebook copy of *Grimm Tidings: A Secret Library Short Read*.

Grimm Tidings can either be read on its own as a stand alone adventure, or between *A New Keeper* and *Call of Kuyr*. You will also be added to my Readers Group where you will be the first to hear about more giveaways.

Thanks again for reading along.

The books are calling...

Don't miss *Call of Kuyr*, book two in The Secret Library series!

Made in the USA
Las Vegas, NV
31 May 2022